Fia and the Butterfly

Fia and the Butterfly

7 Stories for Character Education

Lonnetta M. Taylor-Gaines

CEP

Character Education Press

Sarasota, FL 34235

www.taylor-gaines.com

ISBN # 978-0-9795414-0-7
Printed in the United States of America

Printing History
2001 Edition, TGC Press, New York City 10025
2002 Edition, TGC Press, New York City 10025
2005 Edition, RoseDog Books, Pittsburgh, Pennsylvania 15222
2007 Edition, CEP-Character Education Press, Sarasota, FL 34235

Book Design by Babatunde Odesanya, African Studios
Cover Art and Illustrations by Harvey Richards
Proofreading/Copyediting by James McCallum and Pauline Gilbert-Bader

For author's talks or to order additional books, please contact:

Lonnetta M. Taylor-Gaines
The Lorraine Monroe Leadership Institute
361 West 125th Street, Suite 2000
New York, NY 10027
Phone: 212-531-0515 Fax: 212-531-0535

E-mails: lgaines@lmli.org and taylor-gaines@verizon.net

Web site: www.taylor-gaines.com

These stories are a tribute to my mother and to my father

Mrs. Gladys Marie Harris Gaines

September 3, 1921–April 12, 1982

and

Mr. Lonnie William Gaines, Jr.

August 12, 1922–August 16, 2005

Thank you for the love. Thank you for the discipline.

Thank you for the values.

And they are dedicated to the memory of four little girls

Addie Mae Collins, Denise McNair,

Carole Robertson, and Cynthia Wesley

who were murdered in the

Sixteenth Street Baptist Church in

Birmingham, Alabama

on Sunday, September 15, 1963.

Contents

Additional Information

LMLI
Lorraine Monroe Leadership Institute
361 West 125th Street, Suite 2000
New York, NY 10027

September 15, 2007

Dear Reader,

Do you believe in magic? I hope so, because you are about to enter a very special, magical world. You are about to travel in time and space. You will meet Fredericka Inez Anderson—Fia—an 11-year-old African-American girl who lives during the year 1963. Fia has some of the same joys and some of the same problems that you may have in your life—she has to meet new friends at her new school, she doesn't like the way she looks, and she just hates her school uniform! In addition, because she lives during the time of the Civil Rights Movement, Fia has an unusual problem, too. She's afraid to go to church!

Travel with Fia as she learns lessons about life and about herself. Meet Fia's wise friend who teaches her these lessons. Answer the Questions for Readers and complete the Character Development Activities in order to learn your own lessons . . .

. . . and discover the magical powers of reading and your own imagination. You'll be glad you did!

Sincerely,
Lonnetta M. Taylor-Gaines
Author

The Stories

"I have a dream that my
four children will one day
live in a nation where they
will not be judged by the
color of their skin but by the
content of their character."

Dr. Martin Luther King, Jr.

Introduction

Fia Feels Unhappy

Setting: Louisville, Kentucky and Fia's Imagination

Fredericka Inez Anderson—or Fia as she likes to be called—was feeling very unhappy. "Eleven years old has got to be the hardest age in the world," Fia thought, "so why would my parents choose this time to move to a new city?"

"I want to go home!" Fia said to her mother over and over again.

"You are home, Fia," her mother responded patiently. "Louisville is our new home."

"I want to go back to Mobile," Fia whined.

"That's not possible, Fia," her mother replied.

"Then I want to go to Birmingham and live with my grandmother," Fia retorted.

Passing by, her father said, "Out of the question!" and that ended that.

"They can make me move here, but they can't make me

like it," Fia thought angrily, looking at herself in the bathroom mirror. She didn't like what she saw. "Look at my lips. They're much too big!" Fia practiced a tight-lipped smile to make her lips look smaller. She tugged at her collar and then tried to tuck her neck down into her torso. It didn't work. "Nothing can hide this long neck," she said.

"I want to be pretty," Fia said out loud.

Her mother overheard her and said, "Pretty is as pretty does."

"I know, Mother, you always say that! But I want to look pretty!"

"Fia, my dear, you are pretty! You are my pretty little girl."

Well, that didn't count at all! Fia thought, "I don't look like any of the girls or women I see in the magazines. I don't look like any of the people I see on TV, and I don't look like the girls the boys call pretty at school. So I'm not pretty and that's that."

Fia turned her attention to her hair. "Now here's another problem." She combed her straightened hair over to the left, then she combed it to the right, then she pushed it up to form a little bird's nest at the top of her head. "If I had good hair, I wouldn't straighten it at all," Fia thought. "I would cut my hair down close to my head and that would be that! No more hair problems for me!"

She didn't know that she did have good hair. In 1963, nobody thought that kinky hair was good hair, not even Fia's mother. "Who says that some hair is good and some hair isn't, anyhow?" Fia said to herself as she used a headband to push her hair away from her face.

One day, Fia overheard her mother and father talking quietly to each other after work. They were in the kitchen as usual. Fia's mother was wearing a pink apron with colorful flowers and golden yellow butterflies embroidered around the bottom. She was heating up the baked chicken, collard greens, and candied yams from the day before yesterday for tonight's dinner and making a fresh salad with lettuce, tomatoes, and cucumbers. "Frederick, I think Fia is beginning to adjust to the move," Fia's mother said softly.

"Humph!" Fia's dad responded. He was studying to take the test to become a postal clerk. Fia's dad was a mail carrier who was determined to get a job inside the post office away from the cold Louisville winters. He was tossing practice envelopes by number code into shoeboxes that he had lined up on the kitchen table.

Fia's mother persisted, "Fia doesn't talk about going to live with Mama in Birmingham anymore. I think she's adjusting to the move."

"I knew she'd adjust," Fia's dad replied. "We just had to give her time, Inez. Time is a great healer." Having said that, he kept on studying for his postal examination.

In the next room, Fia was looking out of the dining room window. Snow cloaked everything, turning the bushes and trees into fantastic sculptures. Low-hanging icicles looked like magical rainbows, as they melted in the late-afternoon sun. It was beautiful. "Fia, why don't you go outside and play?" her mother called from the kitchen.

"And break my neck on the icy sidewalks?" Fia snapped back. Her mother sighed and continued to prepare dinner.

"No place is safe anymore," Fia thought. She unlocked her diary and picked up the newspaper article that she kept hidden away there. She unfolded the article carefully and, for the 100th time, she read:

> *September 15—Four Little Girls Killed*
> On Sunday morning, September 15, 1963, in Birmingham, Alabama, a group of terrorists threw a powerful bomb into the basement of the all-Negro Sixteenth Street Baptist Church. Sunday School was in session. The explosion instantly killed 11-year-old Denise McNair along with Addie Mae Collins, Cynthia Wesley, and Carole Robertson, all 14 years old. Scores of others were injured. The terrorists were striking out against Negroes who were marching to protest the system of unequal education for their children. In an effort to stop the Civil Rights Movement, four little girls were killed.

"Four little girls killed in Sunday School! Negro girls like me, killed in church, killed in Birmingham where my grandmother lives!" Fia tucked the newspaper article back into her diary. "No place is safe anymore."

School was the only place that felt predictable. Fia loved school, and here in Louisville the teachers were so much fun! They gave tons of assignments that kept Fia up late at night studying and searching through the dictionary. Back home in Alabama, Fia's friends thought she was crazy because she loved books so much. "Fia's coming over," her cousins would say. "Let's hide the books so she'll play with us."

In this new city, books were Fia's company and every new word was like a new friend. "I wish I could learn more about these words," Fia thought. "The dictionary isn't enough. I wish I could see these new words and really understand them."

Fia loved to dream about words. She especially liked daydreaming on the school bus. The sound of the snow chains on the tires would lull her into a peaceful dream space. In Fia's imagination, she wasn't on a bus at all. She was playing with all the new ideas and new words she was learning in school. Fia smiled as she pulled out her assignment book. On the cover of her book was a drawing of a big, beautiful butterfly that she had found in an issue of the *National Geographic* magazine. Fia had cut the butterfly out carefully and pasted it on the cover of her book. Every time she took out her assignment book, Fia smiled. She loved butterflies!

She opened her book to the homework assignment from her English class. She looked at the list of words to learn—*marvelous, sanctuary, majestic, amazing, awesome, serene, sublime* . . . Fia reread the definitions she had copied from the dictionary. Then she repeated each word to herself, whispering softly. Next, she took out her notebook and began her writing assignment. "Marvelous," she whispered to herself with a smile. "I know a sentence for that word!"

Fia wriggled her fingers under the sleeve of her coat so she could touch the soft wool of the new jacket her mother had made for her. It was her new school uniform. "Why do we have to wear these uniforms?" Fia asked her mother. "We didn't have to . . ."

"I know, Fia," her mother completed her sentence, speaking over the straight pins in her mouth. "You didn't have to wear school uniforms in Mobile. But wait until you see how pretty you look in this jacket," her mother said, pinning the hem to just the right length.

Fia had to agree. The jacket did make her look grown up. But why couldn't it be a nice pastel color—pink or sky blue or lavender—instead of this dull navy blue?

Fia wrote, "My new jacket with its bright, shiny buttons is marvelous!" Now on to the next sentence, she thought smugly. Her confidence faded as she looked at the next word on her list—*sanctuary*. Fia repeated the dictionary definition: "A safe place."

"What's a good sentence for that?" she wondered, nibbling her pencil eraser.

Suddenly, Fia was startled to attention as she heard the other students chanting loudly, "Gooseneck! Gooseneck!" She turned around and was surprised to see that everyone was pointing at her! "Gooseneck! Gooseneck! Fia's got a gooseneck!" Upset, Fia ran to the front of the bus and jumped off at the next stop. "Gooseneck! Gooseneck! Fia's got a gooseneck!" She could still hear their voices as the bus pulled away.

"Why did my parents move to this place?" Fia thought angrily. "I want to go home!" Fia hesitated. "Speaking of home, I wonder where I am now?" she worried. "I probably shouldn't have gotten off the bus," she thought as she walked gingerly on the slippery sidewalk. "Maybe if I run,

I can catch the bus at the next stop." Fia began running when—"WHOOPS!"—she slipped on a patch of ice and fell—WHAMMO!—to the ground. And there she lay, alone on the icy-cold sidewalk.

But Fia was neither alone nor cold in her mind's world. In her dream, Fia lay on a fluffy, white cloud that floated over a lush land of rich, dark earth from which grew leafy green trees and straw-colored grasses. Fia stretched her arms and her legs and rolled over on the billowy cloud to make herself more comfortable. Much to her astonishment, she saw an incredibly beautiful butterfly!

The butterfly looked like the sun rising in an early-morning sky, with outstretched wings—golden yellow with lovely lavender and soft-red highlights—that shimmered with the radiance of precious jewels. The butterfly reminded Fia of the picture on her assignment book, except this butterfly was different from any butterfly Fia had ever seen. She was much larger, for one thing, with a cloud-like body, a human face, kind eyes, and a gentle smile. Amazingly, this butterfly could even talk!

"Well, hello young lady. And who are you?" the butterfly asked Fia in a soft, musical voice. Actually, the butterfly knew exactly who Fia was, but she also understood the value of formal introductions.

"My name is Fredericka Inez Anderson, but everybody calls me Fia," she responded politely. "What is your name, Miz Butterfly?" Fia inquired.

"Well, Fredericka Inez—oh!—I mean Fia," the butterfly corrected herself. "I am Miz Beatrice Louise Butterfly, but you may call me Nana Bea—like a honey bee," she said in her sweet, rich voice.

"Nana!" said Fia, "But that's what I call my grandmother."

"I know," said Nana Bea.

"I'm pleased to meet you, Nana Bea," said Fia. She moved closer to the beautiful butterfly. Fia felt safe.

"I'm pleased to meet you, Fia," Nana Bea responded.

"Where am I, Nana Bea?" Fia asked.

"Well, my dear," Nana Bea said softly, "Our cloud is floating over the continent of Africa, the land of your ancestors. Right below us is the country of Kenya in East Africa. '*Bless, O Lord, our Mother, Africa,*' " Nana Bea sang softly.

"Africa? Kenya? This is very strange," said Fia. "How did I get here, Nana Bea?" Fia asked, stretching her body long so she could peek over the edge of the cloud.

"I'll tell you, Fia," Nana Bea said soothingly. "You came here on the wings of your wishes. You came here through the power of your dreams."

"Why am I here, Nana Bea?" Fia asked.

"Fia, you are here to find answers to some of your questions. You are here to see a vision of your future. Welcome, my child," said Nana Bea. And so it began.

"Fia," said Nana Bea, "First, I want you to learn seven new words."

"New words!" said Fia, sitting up straight.

"Yes, Fia," Nana Bea said. "Listen!"

Umoja, Kujichagulia

Ujima, Ujamaa, Nia, Kuumba, Imani!

Umoja, Kujichagulia
Ujima, Ujamaa, Nia, Kuumba, Imani!

Fia liked the sound, the rhythm of these words, and her body swayed from side to side as Nana Bea chanted:

Umoja, Kujichagulia
*Ujima, Ujamaa, Nia, Kuumba, Imani!**

"Oh my! What language is that, Nana Bea?" Fia asked excitedly.

"*Kiswahili,*" Nana Bea replied. "*Kiswahili* is one of the languages commonly spoken in the country of Kenya."

"What do those words mean, Nana Bea?" Fia asked. Meanwhile, she was thinking, "Hey! I don't care where I am and it doesn't even bother me that I'm talking to a butterfly. I'm learning new words! This is fun!"

"Fia," Nana Bea responded, "Those words are *Kwanzaa* words. Each word represents a principle—a value—and each principle comes with a story that will teach you important lessons about life. Are you ready to hear the seven stories, Fia?"

Fia sat up straight, her eyes shining brightly. "What's first, Nana Bea?"

**See the section "Information about Kwanzaa" for a pronunciation guide and translations for these words.*

Questions for Readers from **The Introduction**

Discuss the questions below.
Write your responses to each question in two or three sentences.

1. What does the word *principle* mean? At the end of the Introduction how does Nana Bea tell Fia she will use the seven *Kwanzaa* principles to teach her important lessons about life?

2. Why is Fia feeling unhappy? List three to five reasons.

3. What real-life event occurred during the Civil Rights Movement that is making Fia feel unsafe? On what date did that event occur?

4. The **Introduction** is named “Fia Feels Unhappy.” If you had to give the **Introduction** another name, what would you name it?

5. What was the sequence of events that led to Fia’s dream? What happened first? What happened next? Then what happened? (Begin with Fia’s family moving from Mobile, Alabama to Louisville, Kentucky.)

6. Why does Fia end up floating on the cloud with Nana Bea? List as many reasons as you can—at least three! Then underscore what you think is the most important reason.

7. What are two or three differences and two or three similarities for Fia between Mobile, Alabama and Louisville, Kentucky?

8. What do you think about Fia's problems? Do Fia's problems remind you of your own problems or the problems of one of your friends? Why or why not?

9. Fia loves to read books and to learn new words! How do you feel about reading books and learning new words? Why?

10. What principles do you expect to learn about through the stories in *Fia and the Butterfly?* How do you think these principles will help you to lead a better life? Make a chart with two columns. Use the Table of Contents to write the name of each principle that you will learn about in *Fia and the Butterfly.* (Each story is named after a principle.)

    In the second column, write one or two sentences that describe how you think each principle will help you to lead a better life. ***Bonus:*** *Make a third column and leave it blank. When you finish reading each story, use the third column to write a new idea about the importance of that principle to you in your life.*

11. What two or three lessons does Fia learn in the **Introduction**?

12. What is the most important lesson for *you* in the **Introduction**? Why?

A Saying to Remember for
The Unity Story

I am one with the world.
I cherish and care for the earth.

Fia and the Butterfly: 7 Stories for Character Education
Dr. Lonnetta M. Taylor-Gaines

The Unity Story

Elephants at the Water Hole

Setting: The Mwaluganje Elephant Sanctuary, Kwale District, Kenya

"F**ia, this first** story will help you to think differently about your new school," said Nana Bea.

"Nana Bea, everybody at school knows each other. I'm the only one who's new." Fia sighed. As Nana Bea and Fia talked, their cloud floated over tall mountains and deep, cavernous valleys. Fia looked down in amazement.

"A lot of those trees look like the trees I see back home," she said to Nana Bea. "This doesn't look anything like the Africa we see on TV on Saturday mornings. Where's the jungle?"

Nana Bea smiled. "You're not looking at something somebody made up for TV or the movies, Fia."

"What's down there, Nana Bea?" Fia asked.

"That's the Mwaluganje Elephant Sanctuary, Fia," Nana Bea responded.

"Oh!" Fia exclaimed. "Sanctuary! That's one of my new words from school."

"I know, Fia," said Nana Bea. "During your visit to Kenya you will see many of your school words. You will understand these words in a new way. That was your wish, wasn't it?"

"Yes, Nana Bea, it's like magic! It's so beautiful," said Fia. "It's—it's sublime," she said, bravely trying out another new word.

"Look, Fia. Look down at the water hole," said Nana Bea. Fia leaned over the edge of the cloud and gasped as she saw a huge bull elephant, tall and mountain-like, bending to drink from the water hole. "Now look at that small hill beyond the water hole," Nana Bea instructed. Fia looked. She saw a line of elephants coming down the winding pathway. The elephants moved their bulky bodies delicately through the trees. "Now watch," Nana Bea said.

Fia watched the arriving line of elephants approach the water hole. Then as the bull elephant looked up from his drinking, the other elephants stopped. Fia wondered what would happen next. The bull elephant waved his trunk. Then the first elephant in the line waved his trunk, too. "Oh!" Fia whispered. "They are saying hello to each other. They are so polite!" Then there was a moment of incredible stillness. The arriving elephants and the bull elephant at the water hole were absolutely motionless. Even the wind paused. Fia held her breath.

Then she exhaled as the arriving line of elephants began to move again, slowly joining the bull elephant at the water hole. The elephants shared the water. They relaxed together in the warm sunshine. The mother elephants sprayed water on themselves and on their children. It was very peaceful.

"How serene they are," said Fia. "Is it always like that, Nana Bea?"

"Not all of the time, Fia. Sometimes the meetings are quite different."

Fia leaned closer to Nana Bea, her eyes alert with interest.

She was thinking about how she felt in her new school. "Tell me about it, Nana Bea," she said. Nana Bea began.

"**One hot and** sultry summer day, my butterfly friends and I sat on a tree branch, sunning ourselves and watching a herd of elephants drinking and enjoying themselves at the water hole. Up the hill, another herd of elephants slowly made its way down the path. As the new herd of elephants approached, the elephants at the water hole looked up, trunks waving as they sniffed the air. We butterflies could tell that the elephants at the water hole sensed the presence of the others. We wondered what would happen, hoping that the meeting would be a peaceful one.

"Suddenly, one of the cow elephants turned away from the water hole and started running up the hill, moving her bulky body with tremendous force. Then a cow elephant from the arriving herd started running down the hill, moving so fast that the earth shook beneath her feet! We butterflies were feeling a little nervous. We detest violence and it sure looked like those elephants were going to fight! Time stretched long as we watched anxiously.

"Finally, the two elephants reached each other. We butterflies gasped in fearful anticipation. Our wings trembled in fright. But moments later, our wings shook with laughter as the two cow elephants intertwined their willowy trunks in an exuberant embrace. Those elephants did not want to fight. They wanted to hug!"

Fia sighed with relief. She didn't want to hear a story about fighting elephants in this peaceful place. "What happened next, Nana Bea?" Fia asked, stretching her legs out in front of her and wiggling her toes with delight.

"After their high-spirited greeting," Nana Bea continued, "the two female elephants walked together like old friends, leading the arriving herd down to the water hole. There, all of the elephants enjoyed the water together in an atmosphere of peace and kindness. After a while, all of the elephants left, moving out together into the safe world of the Mwaluganje Sanctuary."

"Sanctuary," Fia whispered in quiet awe. "I am actually seeing one of my vocabulary words!"

"Fia, do you know what a sanctuary is?" Nana Bea asked.

Fia sat up straight and quoted the dictionary definition she had memorized in school: "A sanctuary is a safe place."

"Yes, Fia," Nana Bea said. "The Mwaluganje Elephant Sanctuary was created as a safe haven for elephants. Elephants are protected here. No one is allowed to hunt and kill them for their tusks. Outside of the sanctuary, some elephants will fight each other and even attack humans. But here in the Mwaluganje Sanctuary, the elephants know they are safe. Here, they can live together in unity—in Umoja."

"Umoja," Fia repeated softly.

"**Fia, do you** know that school is your sanctuary?" Nana Bea asked. "You don't have to feel afraid in your new school."

"They called me gooseneck," Fia said softly.

"Fia, maybe they were just trying to get you to look at them—to come out of your daydreams about words and to see the people around you. Remember that elephant greeting that looked like a fight? Things are not always what they seem."

"No one has ever called me names before," Nana Bea.

"It is not what you are called but what you answer to—what you answer to—that's what really matters. Remember that, Fia."

"I don't like it there, Nana Bea," Fia declared. "I want to move back home where I know everyone."

"Fia, wherever you are is your home," said Nana Bea

gently. "That is the meaning of *Umoja*, the first principle. *Umoja* means Unity—you are one with the world." Fia wrinkled her brow in confusion.

"These are big ideas, Fia," Nana Bea said, "and you will keep thinking about them for a very long time. Right now, just look at the beauty of the elephant sanctuary. Feel its peace."

"Nana Bea, when I look at the elephant sanctuary, I don't care about their name-calling," Fia said with quiet astonishment.

Nana Bea fluttered her wings in agreement.

"Why, Nana Bea? Why does it make me feel better when I look at the trees and the flowers and the sky?"

"Fia, when you look at nature, you awaken the peace that dwells within you. Keep your eyes open to what Mother Nature has to teach you, Fia. You are one with the world."

"I am one with the world," Fia repeated softly.

"Yes, Fia, that's why it is so important to cherish and care for the earth. That's why it is so important to have reverence for life. The earth is our sanctuary, Fia."

Fia took a deep breath. She looked at the blue sky. She looked at the cottony-white clouds. She looked at the bright light of the early-morning sun shining through the leafy green branches of the trees. And slowly, Fia began to smile.

"Thank you, Nana Bea," she whispered.

Questions for Readers from **The Unity Story**

Discuss the questions below.
Write your responses to each question in two or three sentences.

1. What does the word *sanctuary* mean? What is the setting for **The Unity Story?**

2. What does Fia say about the trees in the elephant sanctuary? What does Nana Bea say to Fia in response? Did reading this conversation change any of your ideas about believing something just because you see it on TV? Why or why not?

3. At the beginning of the story, when the new elephants approach the water hole where the bull elephant is drinking, what does the bull elephant do? What does the first elephant in the line do? Why? How do the elephants behave when they arrive at the water hole? What two or three lessons can we learn from these elephants that we can use in our daily lives?

4. **The Unity Story** is named "Elephants at the Water Hole." If you had to give this story another name, what would you name it?

5. In the second part of the story, what makes you think the two cow elephants are going to fight? What happens first? What happens next? Then what happens?

6. Why are the elephants inside the sanctuary so peaceful? Why are the elephants outside of the sanctuary not always so peaceful? What lesson(s) do the elephants in the sanctuary teach us as human beings about how we can create peace in our homes, schools, and communities?

7. In what two or three ways can you compare and contrast how the elephants in the sanctuary treat each other with how people treat each other in our families, in our neighborhoods, and in the world?

8. What do you think Nana Bea means by the statement, "It's not what you are called but what you answer to"? How can you apply this statement in your daily life?

9. Nana Bea tells Fia that she feels better when she looks at nature because looking at nature awakens ". . . the peace that dwells within you." In your opinion, what are other reasons that looking at nature can help a person who is upset to feel better? What two or three things make you feel better when you are feeling upset?

10. What 5 to 7 words, phrases, and/or images in the story make you feel peaceful when you read them or think about them? Sketch a picture of a water hole. Write or draw your peaceful words, phrases, and/or images inside of your water-hole sketch. Remember your water-hole drawing the next time you feel upset.

11. What two or three lessons does Fia learn in **The Unity Story?**

12. What is the most important lesson for *you* in **The Unity Story**? Why?

CHARACTER DEVELOPMENT ACTIVITIES FOR **THE UNITY STORY**

A Saying to Remember

I am one with the world. I cherish and care for the earth.

1. Copy the saying to remember for **The Unity Story**. Put the saying in a special place.

2. Memorize the saying and think about what it means to you.

3. Write a 5- to 8-sentence paragraph that describes how you relate the saying to your own life. Include the following in your paragraph:

   a. What this saying means to you

   b. How you will use this saying to improve yourself in one or more of the following areas: your health, your schoolwork, your attitude, your thoughts and feelings about yourself, your relationships with others, and/or your daily behavior

   Share your paragraph with an encouraging friend or with a supportive adult.

4. Make a list of real-world tasks that you can undertake in order to make the lessons you learned in **The Unity Story** a reality in your life. See the starter list below for ideas.

   a. Enjoy nature. Even if you live in a city, take the time to look at the trees, flowers, and the sky. Make notes about your observations and experiences with nature.
   b. Recycle.
   c. Respect common areas (parks, buses, subways, schoolyards, playgrounds, etc.). Encourage your friends to respect these areas, too.
   d. Make posters to remind others to take care of the environment. (Note: Planet Earth is our entire environment—it's not just the trees and the ground. It includes the sidewalks, the streets, our homes, and our schools, too.)
   e. Make it a personal habit to be kind, polite, and respectful to others. Simple words and phrases like *please, thank you, excuse me, good morning, good afternoon, good evening,* and *have a nice day* can make life more pleasant for everyone.

5. Take action on the real-world tasks on your list. Record your experiences in a special journal.

Character Development Reminder

Think about it! **When you are kind to others and considerate of their feelings, it not only helps them; it helps you, too. Remember, being polite and practicing good manners will help to make you a better person—today and in the future.**

A Saying to Remember for
The Self-Determination Story

I develop my talents and abilities. I grow into my own best self.

Fia and the Butterfly: 7 Stories for Character Education
Dr. Lonnetta M. Taylor-Gaines

The Self-Determination Story

Why Millipedes are Blind

Setting: The Mwaluganje Elephant Sanctuary, Kwale District, Kenya

"**Fia, do you** know anyone who likes practical jokes?" Nana Bea asked.

Fia smiled. "Oh, yes! My Uncle Bubba loves practical jokes."

"Tell me about him, Fia."

"Uncle Bubba is always teasing," Fia said with a smile. "Like, he might give you a can of peanuts to open, but you know you'd better open that can slowly. You might think you're going to eat peanuts, but a toy snake might jump out at you instead!"

"Your Uncle Bubba reminds me of the tricksters in some of my favorite stories, Fia," Nana Bea said. "Tricksters keep you on your toes. They remind you to be alert so you can practice *Kujichagulia*. *Kujichagulia* is the second principle. It means self-determination."

Then out of the blue, Nana Bea asked a question. "Fia, what is your main worry?"

Fia rubbed her hand on the back of her neck and looked away. "I guess I should say something about my family or about the Civil Rights Movement," she said.

"No, Fia," Nana Bea said softly. "I want you to tell me something about yourself. I want to hear what's really on your mind."

Fia was quiet. Nana Bea folded her wings and waited patiently. Then she asked again. "Tell me, Fia, what do you think about most of the time?"

"Nana Bea, do you really want to know?" Fia asked softly.

"I do, Fia."

Fia paused for a minute. Then she took a deep breath, looked at Nana Bea, and blurted, "I think about being popular. That's what I think about!" Fia looked away again.

"Fia, my dear, most young people want to be popular," Nana Bea said.

"But it's really hard for me. I'm new at my school and I feel like I don't belong, like I don't fit in," Fia said. "I'm always on the outside," she continued. "I'd give anything to be popular."

"Listen to yourself, Fia. You just said you'd give anything to be popular. Surely you don't mean that."

"That is what I mean, Nana Bea!"

"Then, Fia," said Nana Bea firmly, "I want you to listen closely to this second story." Fia folded her arms and wrinkled her brows. She moved as close to the edge of the cloud as she dared.

"Look, Fia, crawling there near your feet," Nana Bea said suddenly. "Do you see that millipede?"

"Goodness!" Fia jumped nervously. She moved very quickly to the center of the cloud. "How did that millipede get up here, Nana Bea?"

"She's a friend of mine," Nana Bea said, smiling at the

shiny millipede, which to Fia looked like a small black garden snake. "Don't worry about Missy Millipede, Fia. She won't hurt you. She can't even see you. She's blind," Nana Bea said dryly.

"I'll bet you know how she got that way," Fia said, tucking her feet and legs very close to her body.

"I do," said Nana Bea. "Listen closely to this story, Fia."

"**Long, long ago**, Missy Millipede was one of the prettiest little crawling creatures in the world. She was as round as a young sapling and as black and sparkly as the late-night sky. She could crawl fast-fast to wherever she wanted to go and roll her thousand legs underneath her as neat as a pin when she wanted to stop.

"And that wasn't all. Missy Millipede had magnificent eyes. She could see things that were nearby and she could see things that were far away. Her eyes were pretty to look at, too. Missy Millipede had a kind heart and she had several very nice friends.

"But Missy Millipede wanted more than that. She wanted everyone to like her. She wanted to be popular. 'I'd give anything to be popular, especially with Snake,' Missy Millipede told Cricket. Cricket was Missy Millipede's best friend.

"Now, everyone knows that crickets are musicians, but not everyone knows that there are words to the songs they sing. Every time crickets chirp, they are singing:

Think, think, think! Think before you act!
Think beyond the moment. Think before you act!

"So when Missy Millipede told Cricket she was interested in Snake, Cricket chirped, 'You had better think about that!

You just stay away from Snake, do you hear me, Missy?' But Missy Millipede didn't listen to Cricket. All Missy Millipede cared about was being popular."

"**Early one morning,** Missy Millipede was crawling through some high grasses, rubbing her black skin against the blades to bring up the shine (Missy Millipede spent a lot of time on her looks) when whom should she encounter but Snake.

" 'What luck!' Missy Millipede thought, buffing her skin a bit more even though Snake was as blind as a bat and couldn't see how she looked. Now Snake may have been blind, but no one could deny that he was handsome. Snake was strong and sleek. He had pretty designs on his skin. Missy Millipede thought that Snake was quite wonderful. She loved the way Snake hissed when he spoke and the way he slithered when he moved. She watched with admiration as Snake glided closer.

" 'Good morning, Snake,' said Missy Millipede, sidling up to Snake and placing her body close to his. 'Are you having a nice day?'

" 'Yessss!' Snake hissed in reply. 'I'm having a marvelousssss day, Missssy.'

" 'Oh, I'm so glad to hear that, Snake,' said Missy Millipede with a little giggle.

" 'There's just one little difficulty, though,' Snake continued.

" 'Oh? What's wrong, Snake?' inquired Missy Millipede.

" 'My mother asked me to run an errand for her. I have to go to the other side of the mountain,' Snake said. 'If I could only see, I'd be able to get there and back so much more quickly. Will you help me, Missssy?'

" 'How can I help you, Snake?' Missy Millipede asked.

" 'Well, Missssy,' Snake continued smoothly, 'I would be

ever so grateful if you would lend me your eyes—not for long—just for the afternoon. I'll give them right back to you when I return,' Snake said, like he was asking for the time of day and not for something as essential as Missy Millipede's eyes.

" 'Well, Snake, I don't know if I should,' Missy Millipede said slowly.

"Cricket couldn't believe that her friend was even thinking about letting Snake have her eyes. Cricket chirped loudly:

Think, think, think! Think before you act!
Think beyond the moment. Think before you act!

" 'Maybe you're right, Cricket,' Missy Millipede said slowly. 'Let's go.' "

"When Snake heard Missy Millipede getting ready to leave, he knew he had to think fast! Then he heard the baby ostriches running by—whisk! whisk! whisk!—and he got an idea.

'Missssy, my dear,' Snake said, 'the ostriches are giving a dance concert tonight. After I return your eyes, why don't we go to that concert together? We'll get a good seat right up front and you can tell me everything that's happening on the stage. Come on, Missssy,' Snake wheedled. 'It's just a loan.'

"Cricket chirped desperately:

Think, think, think! Think before you act!
Think beyond the moment. Think before you act!

"But instead of listening to Cricket, Missy Millipede thought, 'Wow! I'm going to go out with Snake! After tonight, I'll be Miss Popularity!' She turned to Snake. 'Now, what is it you want, Snake? You say you want to borrow my eyes?'

" 'Oh, just for a little while, Missssy. I'll return them in plenty of time for us to go to the concert tonight,' Snake said. 'Wait right here under this tree. I'll be back before you feel the heat of the noonday sun,' Snake said to gullible Missy Millipede.

"Missy Millipede's friend Cricket chirped frantically! 'No! No! No! Don't do it, Missy!'

Think, think, think! Think before you act!
Think beyond the moment. Think before you act!

"But Missy Millipede didn't think about what might happen next. All she could think about was having fun and feeling popular; and so, she gave Snake her eyes!

" 'Don't worry, Cricket,' Missy Millipede said to her distressed friend. 'It's just a loan. Snake will come back like he said he would. You'll see. He'll come back. Just wait with me here under this tree, Cricket. He'll come back.' "

"And did he come back, Nana Bea? Did Snake come back with Missy Millipede's eyes?" Fia asked anxiously.

"Now, Fia, what do you think?" Nana Bea asked. "Do you really think Snake returned with Missy Millipede's eyes?"

"No, Nana Bea," Fia said sadly.

"No, he did not!" Nana Bea agreed, saying:

And that is why millipedes are blind to this day,
They used to have eyes, but they just gave them away.
Remember these words just as long as you live—
Never lend something that you would not choose to give.
And understand this lesson above all else—
Nothing is more precious than your own essential self.

"**Fia,**" **Nana Bea** said firmly, "I want you to remember Missy Millipede's story. Beware of quick talkers. When it's time to make a decision, remember Cricket's advice. Think before you act! Think beyond the moment and then . . ."

"Oh!" Fia said with a little gasp.

"Yes, Fia?" Nana Bea inquired, tilting her head to the side. "What is it?"

"You said 'think beyond the moment,' Nana Bea, and Cricket said it, too. I just remembered something! Miss Daniels, our physical education teacher at school, she says the same thing. 'Think beyond the moment.' She's always saying that, Nana Bea!"

"What else does she say, Fia?"

Fia bowed her head, hunched her shoulders, and placed her hands under her chin. She was trying to remember. Then her face lit up. "Miss Daniels says, 'If you're tempted to look at TV or talk on the telephone instead of doing your homework, then you need to think beyond the fun you might have in the moment. You have to think about how you need a good education for your future.' "

"Your teacher is right, Fia!"

"She says, 'If a friend asks you to do something that you know is wrong, don't do it. Think! Think beyond the moment and then say no.' "

"Good, Fia," Nana Bea said. "Keep going."

"Well, Miss Daniels says that we have to be responsible for ourselves even though we're still young. Miss Daniels says that we have to take good care of our health by getting plenty of rest and exercising every day. 'Running around on the playground counts as exercise,' she says.

" 'That's not too hard,' we tell her. 'We like to play and exercise!'

"And then Miss Daniels says that we have to drink lots of

water and eat the right foods, like lots of fruits and vegetables and not too many sweets and greasy foods.

" 'Now wait a minute, Miss Daniels!' we tell her. 'That's not easy! You're asking us to give up some of our favorite foods!'

"But Miss Daniels tells us, 'You have to eat to live, not live to eat!' "

Nana Bea chuckled. "Go on, Fia."

"And," Fia continued slowly, "Miss Daniels says that we girls should never give ourselves away. She says we have to keep ourselves whole. I'm not sure I know what she means by that . . ."

"Fia, those are *Kujichagulia* lessons," Nana Bea said. "*Kujichagulia* is a lifelong journey. The first step of that journey is learning to think for yourself. Think, Fia—it's not an illegal activity," Nana Bea joked.

"Tell me again, Nana Bea, what does *Kujichagulia* mean?"

"*Kujichagulia* means self-determination," said Nana Bea. "The principle of *Kujichagulia* reminds you to develop your talents and abilities so you can grow into your own best self. You are special, Fia. No one else in the whole world is exactly like you.

"Don't worry about being popular," Nana Bea continued softly. "Don't try to fit in with the crowd. Remember, Fia, you are known by the company you keep. Choose friends who are serious about school like you are. That's all you need, Fia, a circle of serious friends."

Fia felt grateful. "Thank you, Nana Bea," she said quietly. Fia knew that she would be learning the lessons of *Kujichagulia* for the rest of her life.

Questions for Readers from **The Self-Determination Story**

Discuss the questions below.
Write your responses to each question in two or three sentences.

1. What does the word *errand* mean? How does Snake want Missy Millipede to help him with his errand?

2. What does Fia tell Nana Bea is her main worry? What does Fia say that makes Nana Bea want to tell her another story?

3. What does Cricket keep chirping to Missy Millipede? Why is this saying important for Missy Millipede? Why is this saying important for everyone?

4. **The Self-Determination Story** is named "Why Millipedes Are Blind." If you had to give this story another name, what would you name it?

5. At first, it seems as if Missy Millipede is going to listen to Cricket's advice and ignore Snake. What does Snake say to Missy Millipede to convince her to give him her eyes? What happens next? What happens after that?

6. How did Missy Millipede's poor judgment lead to poor results in the story? Give two or three examples that illustrate how acting without thinking can create problems in everyday life.

7. What two or three examples does Fia's teacher, Miss Daniels, use to encourage her students to think beyond the moment? How do you compare and contrast Miss Daniels' examples with two or three examples in your own life or in the life of someone you know?

8. In your opinion, what does it mean to be responsible for yourself? Use two or three of Miss Daniels' examples and two or three of your own. Do you think it is important to follow her advice? Why or why not?

9. What advice does Miss Daniels give about eating the right foods? Do you think that her advice is easy to follow? Why or why not?

10. If you were a teacher, what advice would you give to your students in order to encourage them to take good care of their health? Use drawings or magazine cutouts to make a poster that illustrates your advice in an attractive way.

11. What two or three lessons does Fia learn in **The Self-Determination Story?**

12. What is the most important lesson for *you* in **The Self-Determination Story?** Why?

CHARACTER DEVELOPMENT ACTIVITIES FOR **THE SELF-DETERMINATION STORY**

A Saying to Remember

I develop my talents and abilities. I grow into my own best self.

1. Copy the saying to remember for **The Self-Determination Story.** Put the saying in a special place.

2. Memorize the saying and think about what it means to you.

3. Write a 5- to 8-sentence paragraph that describes how you relate the saying to your own life. Include the following in your paragraph:

   a. What this saying means to you

   b. How you will use this saying to improve yourself in one or more of the following areas: your health, your schoolwork, your attitude, your thoughts and feelings about yourself, your relationships with others, and/or your daily behavior

   Share your paragraph with an encouraging friend or with a supportive adult.

4. Make a list of real-world tasks that you can undertake in order to make the lessons you learned in **The Self-Determination Story** a reality in your life. See the starter list below for ideas.

   a. Eat three to five servings of fresh fruits and vegetables every day.
   b. Exercise or play actively for at least one/half hour each day.
   c. Interview two or three leaders in your home, your school, or in your community. Make a list of five to ten lessons that you learned from these leaders. What talents and skills did these leaders develop in order to become successful?
   d. Make a list of five to eight professional careers. Next to each career on your list, describe the skills, education, and training needed to succeed in that career.
   e. Make a collage that illustrates your hopes and dreams for your future.

5. Take action on the real-world tasks on your list. Record your experiences in a special journal.

Character Development Reminder

***Think about it!* It's better to be alone than to be with the wrong crowd. Remember, you are known by the company you keep. Sometimes being alone with yourself is the best company of all!**

A Saying to Remember for
The Collective Work and Responsibility Story

I work well with others.
I am helpful and responsible.

The Collective Work and Responsibility Story

How the Chi Chi Butterflies Got Their Permanent Wings

Setting: The Butterfly Breeding Station at The Bamburi Forest Nature Trails Mombasa, Kenya

F**ia was thinking**, "I wish Nana Bea would tell me a story to make me feel pretty." Then—to Fia's astonishment—Nana Bea said, "How pretty you are, Fia! And you look quite smart in your school uniform."

"Oh, Nana Bea," Fia moaned. "You can't mean that! I don't like anything about the way I look—and I do not like having to wear this boring uniform to school every day!"

"Hush your mouth, Fia," Nana Bea said with a smile. "You sound just like one of our Chi Chi butterflies!"

"What's a chee chee, Nana Bea?"

"A Chi Chi is a young butterfly, Fia, like a teenager. And like many young people, Chi Chi butterflies are not always satisfied with how they look. Look, Fia! Those are Chi Chi butterflies down there," said Nana Bea.

Fia peeked over the edge of the cloud. She saw dozens of butterflies fluttering over a mirror-smooth lake. The butterflies moved with precision, flittering and fluttering from side to side and up and down in fantastic unison. They reminded

Fia of the drill team at her new school. They were together! Moving as one, the Chi Chi's came to rest, folding their wings at exactly the same time.

"Wow!" said Fia. "That was amazing!"

"Nothing amazing about it, Fia," Nana Bea responded. "They're Chi Chi butterflies. That's what they do."

The cloud carrying Nana Bea and Fia moved over the countryside and then floated over the busy city of Mombasa. Fia looked down. It was fascinating to watch the people moving through the streets! Fia saw men and women dressed in suits and carrying briefcases; she also saw people dressed in traditional African clothing, moving gracefully while balancing large baskets on their heads. She saw children dressed in school uniforms with arms full of books. The streets were filled with people who were walking, driving cars and vans, or pushing carts loaded with fruits and vegetables. Everyone moved quickly and with focused purpose, even the children!

As their cloud continued to float over the busy city, Fia lay on her stomach, stretched her arms wide, and pretended she could fly. She smiled happily.

After a while, Fia noticed that their cloud was hovering over a small garden. In the garden were beautiful flowers and huge palm trees with gigantic leaves that stretched up toward the sky like giant green hands. Fia saw a group of colorful butterflies flitting playfully among the flowers.

"More butterflies! This is heaven!" Fia giggled.

"Fia, do you see the Chi Chi butterflies down there?" Nana Bea asked.

"Which ones are they?" Fia inquired.

"Look!" said Nana Bea. "The Chi Chi butterflies are all clustered together. Do you see them? They are all doing the same thing—flittering and fluttering in exactly the same way."

Fia nodded her head briskly. "I see them, Nana Bea!" she said.

"Well," Nana Bea commented, "at least they have stopped changing the look of their wings."

"Oh!" said Fia. "Can butterflies change how their wings look, Nana Bea?"

"Not anymore, Fia," Nana Bea replied with a twinkle in her eyes, "but there was a time when they could."

"Nana Bea," Fia said, smiling with delight, "I feel a story coming on."

Nana Bea smiled, too and began, "Once upon a time, there was a lovely little butterfly village called *Ujima Land. Ujima Land* was filled with lovely flowers of all shapes and colors. Living among those flowers were hundreds and hundreds of beautiful butterflies. The butterflies cared for the flowers. They helped the flowers to grow by carrying pollen from one flower to the other. And the flowers provided nectar to feed the butterflies. The butterflies and the flowers lived together in *Ujima*—in collective work and responsibility—each one helping and caring for the other.

"But one day *Ujima Land* was invaded by predatory birds. The birds attacked the butterflies and ate them. It was terrible!

"The only butterfly safe from the attacking birds was their queen—Queen Esther. Now, Queen Esther had a substance in her body that caused any bird that even so much as nibbled the tip of her wing to topple over and die. Child, let me tell you, those birds were surely afraid of Queen Esther! 'If you see a butterfly with wings like that, keep away!' they chirped. But none of the other butterflies were safe. In order to save their lives, they had to move away.

" 'Come with us, Queen Esther,' the fleeing butterflies said.

" 'No, I have to stay in *Ujima Land*. Someone has to care for the flowers,' Queen Esther replied.

"And so they left Queen Esther all alone in *Ujima Land*. It was very sad."

Fia thought about her grandmother back home.

"**The new land** was not like *Ujima Land* at all. It was cold and there were not as many flowers. The butterflies had a big problem. They had come from a land where there was an abundance of flowers. Now there were only a few. They needed to find a way to share so that they could stay alive.

"One of the butterflies had an idea. 'Let's solve our problem in an orderly fashion. Every butterfly should get in line. Then we can take turns sipping the nectar from the flowers—a little for each one of us,' the butterfly urged. The butterflies lined up diligently, but then Frolicsome Breeze saw them and scattered their butterfly line with just one poof!"

Fia laughed. "Did the butterflies try again, Nana Bea?"

"Oh yes, Fia, they tried several times; but every time the butterflies lined up, Frolicsome Breeze would go 'poof' and the butterflies would float away. Butterflies are wonderful creatures, but we are absolutely no good at making lines!" Nana Bea said with a soft chuckle.

"Then what happened, Nana Bea?"

"Oh, the butterflies tried another idea. 'Let's organize ourselves,' another butterfly suggested. 'If every butterfly family chooses its own type of flower, it will be easier to share, and we'll always know where to go to find food.' This idea worked. Every butterfly family chose its own type of flower to care for and the flowers provided food for the hungry butterflies.

"The Spirit of the Wind was pleased with how the butterflies solved their problem and promised each butterfly family its own distinctive set of wings. 'With permanent wings, you will always be able to recognize each other and your new flower homes.'

"But the young Chi Chi butterflies protested, 'Permanent wings? That sounds like uniforms! We don't want to look the same way every day! That's so B-O-R-I-N-G!'

"So when the Spirit of the Wind gave the other butterflies their permanent wings, the young Chi Chi butterflies hid and refused to accept the gift. Then the Chi Chi butterflies flew to Mirror Lake where they spent most of their time and continued their favorite activity—making up, dressing up, and changing the look of their wings."

Fia adjusted her hair, pulled her skirt down, removed her jacket, and tied it around her shoulders like a cape. "What did the other butterflies think?" she asked.

"Well, Fia," Nana Bea replied, "some of the older butterflies complained. They said, 'Those Chi Chi butterflies are so frivolous. Why do they spend so much time on how they look?'

"But some of their friends disagreed. They said, 'The Chi Chi butterflies are still young, and they have so much potential. Maybe they're not so different from the way we were when we were young. Don't you remember your own Chi Chi days?'

"Then the complaining butterflies wriggled their antennas angrily. 'We were never like these frivolous young Chi Chi butterflies! We were different!' they asserted."

"**One day the** butterfly families were sitting together quietly, experiencing a golden moment of silence. Then, in the silence, they heard the Spirit of the Wind speaking to them in a *still small voice*. 'Something has happened to Queen Esther. The beautiful flowers in Ujima Land are dying. Queen Esther needs you. The flowers need you. Someone must go to help.'

" 'Who will go?' the butterflies asked each other. 'Who will go to help Queen Esther and the flowers?' No one came forward. They were all afraid of the predatory birds. 'Who will go?' they wondered.

"The Chi Chi butterflies huddled together in a corner, whispering to each other, flapping their wings, and wriggling their antennae. Then one of the Chi Chi butterflies came forward, speaking for the rest. 'We will go,' the Chi Chi butterfly said quietly. 'We will go to help Queen Esther.'

" 'Oh!' all of the other butterflies gasped. 'How very brave you are!'

" 'We are not so brave,' the Chi Chi butterflies said. 'We just want to help.' Then they admitted, 'But we're not exactly sure what we should do. How shall we begin?'

" 'That's easy,' one of the elder butterflies said. 'Begin with what you do best. Begin by changing the look of your wings. But this time make your wings look like Queen Esther's wings.'

" 'Of course!' all the butterflies chanted. 'Make your wings look like Queen Esther's wings and you'll trick those predatory birds! Change your wings to look like hers, and you can trick those birds!'

"The Chi Chi butterflies got right to work, making up and dressing up and changing the look of their wings. Finally, everyone agreed that the Chi Chi butterflies' wings looked just like Queen Esther's wings. Now it was time to try their plan.

"Very early the next morning, the Chi Chi butterflies—disguised as Queen Esther—flew off to *Ujima Land*. When they arrived, they flew low, hiding among the flowers, but then they worked up their courage. They had come to help. This was no time to hide. They fluttered their wings and flew high above the wilting flowers, looking for Queen Esther.

They could feel the birds staring at them but the Chi Chi butterflies did not turn back. They kept on flying. And do you know what? Those birds were none the wiser! The birds did not attack the Chi Chi butterflies!

"Finally, the Chi Chi butterflies found Queen Esther. She was so exhausted from trying to care for all of the flowers that she could barely speak. 'Don't worry, Queen Esther,' they said. 'We will take care of you. We will care for the flowers, too.'

" 'Oh, thank you. Thank you for helping,' Queen Esther whispered weakly."

"**After Queen Esther** felt strong again and the flowers were restored, the Chi Chi butterflies flew back to the new land. They had an idea. 'Listen!' they said to the other butterflies, 'Since the disguise worked for us, we think it can work for you, too!'

" 'Okay!' the other butterflies said. 'We'll give it a try.' Then the Chi Chi butterflies helped all the other butterflies to make up and dress up until their wings looked like Queen Esther's wings.

" 'We're going to trick those birds and return to our homeland,' they said."

"Did their plan work, Nana Bea?" Fia asked.

"Oh yes, Fia," Nana Bea said with a broad smile. "The disguised butterflies flew back to *Ujima Land.* The birds saw them, but they couldn't tell which butterflies to eat. All of the butterflies looked like Queen Esther! Those birds were frustrated! And so, defeated by the clever butterflies, the birds flew away, leaving *Ujima Land* for good.

" 'What we have prayed for has come to pass!' said Queen Esther thankfully, leading the butterflies in a dance of praise. As they danced, the butterflies shook off their disguises.

"The elder butterflies praised the young Chi Chi butterflies. 'We knew you were not really frivolous,' they said. 'You worked well with each other. You were helpful and responsible. And you saved Queen Esther and the flowers! Because of you, we have returned to our homeland! You are all quite wonderful!' The elder butterflies continued their joyous dance.

"The Chi Chi butterflies danced, too—fluttering and flittering their wings at the exact same time like they always did. But as the celebration continued, an interesting thing happened. The Chi Chi butterflies stopped moving in unison. One by one, each Chi Chi butterfly began to move in her or his own unique way.

" 'This is truly a day for giving thanks!' exclaimed one of the elder butterflies. 'Our Chi Chi butterflies are growing up!' She turned to the Chi Chi butterflies and asked, 'What lessons have you learned as a result of your experiences?' "

"**After a moment,** one of the Chi Chi butterflies spoke. 'I learned how good it feels to help.'

"Then another Chi Chi butterfly spoke up. 'I learned that even when you feel afraid, you can still take action.'

"Yet another Chi Chi butterfly came forward, looking at the others and speaking slowly. 'You know, we didn't even mind when our wings all looked the same. Making our wings look like Queen Esther's wings kept us safe.'

"Then the Chi Chi butterflies huddled together, whispering to each other. 'At first, we spent a lot of time at Mirror Lake trying to improve our looks. How we looked was more important to us than anything. But when Queen Esther needed us, we changed the look of our wings because we wanted to help. Our wings looked like uniforms but it was all right. It felt so good to be helpful!'

"The Chi Chi butterflies paused. They looked at their wings. They looked at each other. And then they said something very wise. 'Now we understand. What you do is more important than how you look. Goodness is better than beauty.'

" 'What did you say?' asked one of the elder butterflies.

" 'Goodness is better than beauty,' repeated the Chi Chi butterflies. 'What you *do* is more important than how you look!'

"The elder butterflies beamed proudly. 'We knew it would happen,' they said. 'We knew our Chi Chi butterflies would grow up. We just had to give them time.'

"And so," said Nana Bea, "when the Spirit of the Wind offered the Chi Chi butterflies their permanent wings—wings that looked almost like Queen Esther's wings—the Chi Chi butterflies were finally able to accept the gift! Protected by their new wings, the Chi Chi butterflies flew to many places, experiencing the world and helping others, but they always returned to *Ujima Land.*"

"*Ujima Land!* It's this place isn't it, Nana Bea?" Fia asked, looking around at the beautiful multicolored flowers.

"Yes, Fia," Nana Bea replied. "In this place everyone strives to practice *Ujima*—collective work and responsibility. To practice *Ujima* means to work together as a team, to be kind to others, to be helpful, and to be responsible. Do you understand, Fia?"

Fia was silent for quite a while. She was thinking. Fia thought about her school uniform. She thought about all the time she spent in front of the mirror wishing to be pretty. Then she thought about the Chi Chi butterflies and what they learned when they saved *Ujima Land.* Fia's face broke into a smile and she shouted, "Yes!" Fia understood.

Questions for Readers from **The Collective Work and Responsibility Story**

Discuss the questions below.
Write your responses to each question in two or three sentences.

1. What does the word *predatory* mean? What did the predatory birds do to the butterflies in *Ujima Land*?

2. Describe three or four things that Fia saw when she looked down at the busy city of Mombasa. Did Fia's description of the city of Mombasa change any of your ideas about the continent of Africa? Why or why not?

3. What is a Chi Chi butterfly? How could Fia tell which butterflies were Chi Chi butterflies? In what two or three ways do the Chi Chi butterflies remind you of young people in real life?

4. **The Collective Work and Responsibility Story** is named "How the Chi Chi Butterflies Got Their Permanent Wings." If you had to give this story another name, what would you name it?

5. What did the butterflies do first when they tried to solve their problem of having limited food in the new land? What happened? What did they do next? Then what happened? How did they finally solve their problem?

6. Why were the birds afraid to eat Queen Esther? Why were the birds afraid to eat the Chi Chi butterflies and the other butterflies when they returned to *Ujima Land* disguised as Queen Esther?

7. In what two or three ways are the butterflies' permanent wings similar to school uniforms? In what two or three ways are the butterflies' permanent wings different from school uniforms?

8. In your opinion, why were the Chi Chi butterflies finally willing to accept their permanent wings?

9. In your opinion, why was it a sign of becoming more grown up for each Chi Chi butterfly to begin to dance in her or his own unique way? For people, what do you think are three or four signs of growing up? Do you think you are becoming more grown up? Why or why not?

10. In what three or four ways do the butterflies—all of the butterflies—demonstrate their connection and commitment to their butterfly community throughout **The Collective Work and Responsibility Story**? Make a timeline or story map that records all of the major events in **The Collective Work and Responsibility Story** in sequence. Place a star (or other symbol) next to the events that demonstrate the butterflies' connection and commitment to their butterfly community.

11. What two or three lessons does Fia learn in **The Collective Work and Responsibility Story**?

12. What is the most important lesson for *you* in **The Collective Work and Responsibility Story**? Why?

CHARACTER DEVELOPMENT ACTIVITIES FOR THE COLLECTIVE WORK AND RESPONSIBILITY STORY

A Saying to Remember

I work well with others.
I am helpful and responsible

1. Copy the saying to remember for **The Collective Work and Responsibility Story**. Put the saying in a special place.

2. Memorize the saying and think about what it means to you.

3. Write a 5- to 8-sentence paragraph that describes how you relate the saying to your own life. Include the following in your paragraph:

    a. What this saying means to you

    b. How you will use this saying to improve yourself in one or more of the following areas: your health, your schoolwork, your attitude, your thoughts and feelings about yourself, your relationships with others, and/or your daily behavior

    Share your paragraph with an encouraging friend or with a supportive adult.

4. Make a list of real-world tasks that you can undertake in order to make the lessons that you learned in **The Collective Work and Responsibility Story** a reality in your life. See the starter list below for ideas.

    a. Do extra chores around the house without being asked to do them.
    b. Work together with your classmates to keep the hallways of your school clean and free of litter.
    c. Get permission from your parents or guardians to organize a campaign to keep the street you live on free of litter.
    d. Grow flowers and plants to beautify your room, your home, and/or your neighborhood. Take good care of your flowers and plants!
    e. Wear your complete school uniform to school every day. (If your school does not require a uniform, dress like a scholar each day.)

5. Take action on the real-world tasks on your list. Record your experiences in a special journal.

Character Development Reminder

Think about it! **Wearing your uniform (or neat, scholarly clothes) to school every day shows that you are a serious student, ready to make the most of your education. Remember—you are a part of a very special community—the community of scholars!**

A Saying to Remember for
The Cooperative Economics Story

I care and I share.
I aim to increase the
good in the world.

The Cooperative Economics Story

How Mother Nature Makes the Butterfly

Setting: The Tototo Women's Group, Mombasa, Kenya

"N**ana Bea, am** I a Chi Chi?" Fia asked with a knowing smile.

"You certainly are," responded Nana Bea. "A Chi Chi isn't just a young butterfly. A Chi Chi is also any young person in transition. During these important years, Fia, you are beginning to grow into the woman that you will become."

"Then I'm in big trouble because I don't know who that is," Fia replied. "Everybody says to me, 'Be yourself.' But who is that? Who is *myself?*" Fia lamented. "And everything seems to be changing—not just moving to another city and going to a new school. I mean, I'm changing—my body and the way I feel."

"Fia, what you are feeling is Mother Nature beginning to work her miracle in you."

"What does that mean?" asked Fia.

"Fia, how much do you know about butterflies and how

they grow?"

"Well, I know that butterflies start as caterpillars. I know that much," Fia said. "What else is there?"

"I'll tell you, Fia. And as you listen to how Mother Nature makes the butterfly, I want you to think about your own life changes."

Nana Bea began. "First, Mama Butterfly lays her eggs on the underside of the leaves so they will not be spotted by the birds. From the beginning, Mama Butterfly is working with Mother Nature to protect her young. When the time is right, the eggs hatch and out come the fuzzy caterpillars. Mama Butterfly cannot feed her young, but she has placed her eggs where they can find food immediately. The caterpillar's first meal is the leaf that has sheltered it as an egg.

"The caterpillar's main job is to eat. It eats the nearby leaves and then crawls around in its neighborhood looking for more food. Caterpillars are known to be very hungry. Imagine! A caterpillar will eat until it grows too big for its skin! When this happens, it sheds the old skin for new skin and just keeps on eating! After a time," Nana Bea continued, "the caterpillar begins to slow down. Its body is getting ready to undergo a tremendous transformation.

"First, the caterpillar attaches itself to a twig with a sticky, silk-like thread. Then the caterpillar becomes very still and the first transformation begins. The outside of its body becomes hard—like a shell."

"Is it still a caterpillar, Nana Bea?"

"No, it is already becoming a new creature. At this point, it is called a *chrysalis*. The chrysalis hangs on the twig for what seems like a very long time. On the outside, it looks like nothing is happening, but inside, great changes are taking place. Inside, the caterpillar is being transformed. Its caterpillar body is growing smaller. It is developing antennae. It is growing wings! For all of this to happen, the new creature must remain patient. If it becomes impatient and tries to leave the chrysalis too soon, it will die. But for those patient creatures that allow Mother Nature to work her transformative wonders, the reward is great. Those creatures become butterflies," said Nana Bea quietly.

"One day, when the time is right, the chrysalis begins to move as the butterfly within awakens. Then the chrysalis opens and the delicate butterfly emerges. Through the miracle of metamorphosis, Mother Nature has transformed the lowly caterpillar into a glorious butterfly!"

"Like you, Nana Bea," said Fia with wonder.

"And like you too, Fia. Each person possesses the potential to grow, develop, and transform into a new being."

Their cloud floated over the busy city until it came to rest, hovering over a group of stone buildings. A group of women stood outside of the largest building. "Look, Fia," said Nana Bea. "And listen." One of the women spoke.

"We are the women of the Tototo Women's Group. We have come together in order to help each other. We care and we share. We aim to increase the good in the world."

"We care and we share. We aim to increase the good in the world," Fia repeated softly.

"We help each other through our lending club and also through sharing ideas about how we can improve our lives," the woman continued. "Today we dedicate this school which we have built for our children. To build this school, we practiced the principle of *Ujamaa*, which means cooperative economics."

Then another woman spoke: "Now we have a new problem. Our well has run dry. We must save money in order to dig a new well for our village so we can have running water in our homes and in our school."

"What! They don't have running water?" Fia exclaimed. "I thought everyone had running water!"

"No, Fia. Not everyone has running water, not even in your country," Nana Bea responded. "There is so much need in the world. But even though these women have so little, they are increasing what they have through *Ujamaa*—through cooperative economics. The members of the Tototo Women's Group are working together and sharing their resources, trying to create a better world for themselves and for their children."

"I want to help these women," said Fia.

"Good," Nana Bea responded. "But first things first."

"What do you mean by that, Nana Bea?"

"First, Fia, you must develop yourself."

"Develop myself? How, Nana Bea?" Fia asked.

"**Look at the** butterfly and learn," Nana Bea said. "Nourish your body well and take care of your health so that Mother Nature can work her wonders in you. And when it is time to learn, be like the hungry caterpillar! Seek knowledge! Love learning! And read, Fia! Discover the magic in books and reading! And when the winter times of life come—the chrysalis times—trust Mother Nature. Learn to be still. Learn to be patient with the changes."

"Then will I be like the butterfly?" Fia asked.

"Then, Fia, you will become something even more special than a butterfly."

"What could be more special than a butterfly?" Fia asked.

"A woman . . ." said Nana Bea solemnly, ". . . a woman who is educated and independent, who can work for herself and build with others . . . a woman who can practice *Ujamaa*—cooperative economics—and help to make things right!"

Questions for Readers from **The Cooperative Economics Story**

Discuss the questions below.
Write your responses to each question in two or three sentences.

1. What does the word *metamorphosis* mean? What process (or processes) does this word describe in **The Cooperative Economics Story?**

2. What words does Nana Bea use to describe what it means to be a Chi Chi? According to Nana Bea, could a boy or a young man be a Chi Chi? Why?

3. At the beginning of the story Fia says that everything seems to be changing. What three changes does she mention? Do you identify with Fia's changes? Why or why not?

4. **The Cooperative Economics Story** is named "How Mother Nature Makes the Butterfly." If you had to give this story another name, what would you name it?

5. What are the four phases in the life cycle of the butterfly? List and describe the four phases in the order in which they occur.

6. What does Nana Bea say will happen to a butterfly that tries to leave the chrysalis too soon? What two or three other examples—real or imagined—remind you of the chrysalis and the butterfly?

7. How would you compare and contrast the four phases in the life of the butterfly to other phases, for example, seasons of the year, cycles of the moon, levels in school? How would you compare and contrast the four phases in the life of the butterfly to phases in the life of a human being? How is each phase the same? List two or three ways. How is each phase different? List two or three ways.

8. When Fia says she wants to help the women of the Tototo Women's Group, what advice does Nana Bea give to her? Do you agree or disagree with Nana Bea's advice to Fia? Why?

9. What do you think Nana Bea means when she tells Fia to discover the magic in books and reading? Why do you think Nana Bea gives Fia this advice?

10. How can learning about nature and about the experiences of other people help us to learn important life lessons? What are other ways we can learn important lessons about life? Make a chart that illustrates the lessons you have learned in your life so far. Your chart should include a brief explanation of how you learned each lesson. Your chart should also include advice you would give to others as a result of each lesson that you learned.

11. What two or three lessons did Fia learn in **The Cooperative Economics Story?**

12. What is the most important lesson for *you* in **The Cooperative Economics Story?** Why?

Character Development Activities For THE COOPERATIVE ECONOMICS STORY

A Saying to Remember

I care and I share.
I aim to increase the good in the world.

1. Copy the saying to remember for **The Cooperative Economics Story**. Put the saying in a special place.

2. Memorize the saying and think about what it means to you.

3. Write a 5- to 8-sentence paragraph that describes how you relate the saying to your own life. Include the following in your paragraph:

   a. What this saying means to you

   b. How you will use this saying to improve yourself in one or more of the following areas: your health, your schoolwork, your attitude, your thoughts and feelings about yourself, your relationships with others, and/or your daily behavior

   Share your paragraph with an encouraging friend or with a supportive adult.

4. Make a list of real-world tasks that you can undertake in order to make the lessons you learned in **The Cooperative Economics Story** a reality in your life. See the starter list below for ideas.

    a. Save 25% to 50% of the money that you earn or receive as gifts. Put your savings in a bank.
    b. Get help to compute how much money you would have if you kept your savings in the bank at 5% interest until you reach the age of 18.
    c. Set a long-term goal for what you will do with your savings.
    d. Get together with your classmates or friends to research and make a list of good causes that need help, for example the Children's Defense Fund and international causes like UNICEF that help children throughout the world.
    e. Create a Community Service Club with your classmates or friends. Think of ways to earn money as a group (for example, car washes, raffles, talent shows). Donate the money that you earn to a good cause of your choice.

5. Take action on the real-world tasks on your list. Record your experiences in a special journal.

Character Development Reminder

Think about it! **When you save your money, you can pay for things that you need, treat yourself to things that you want, and give to others, too. But don't spend everything! Remember, it's a good idea to develop the habit of saving.**

A Saying to Remember for
The Purpose Story

I value learning.
I get a good education so I can take care of myself and give something back to my family, to my community, and to my Creator.

The Purpose Story

History Lessons from a Storyteller

Setting: The Wema Centre for Children, Mombasa, Kenya

Nana Bea was quiet for a long time but Fia didn't mind. There was so much to think about. Fia thought about the members of the Tototo Women's Group and about how they were trying to make things better for their children.

"In a way, those women are like the people in the Civil Rights Movement," Fia said to herself, thinking about the brave people she saw on the news—people marching arm in arm, standing up against the vicious assaults of attack dogs and skin-tearing water from fire hoses. Those courageous people were marching for justice. They were trying to change the laws that separated the races—but it seemed impossible! "How can marching make things better?" Fia wondered.

Fia felt sad until she remembered a speech her principal gave at an assembly in her school back home in Mobile. "Remember, with faith and hard work all things are possible! You must never give up!" he told them. "Don't forget that our school was named after a man who realized an impossible dream. Mr. Booker T. Washington was born into slavery—but he got an education.

"Now scholars, do you remember what Mr. Washington said about school and studying?" The students responded in unison, quoting Mr. Booker T. Washington who said, "I had the feeling that to get into a schoolhouse and study would be about the same as getting into paradise."

"Yes!" Fia's principal said, smiling at his students. "And scholars, Mr. Washington achieved his goal of getting an education, but as you all know, it wasn't easy! When he was only a boy, he had to work in a salt mine for many hours both before and after school—but that didn't stop him. He still went to school! In order to go to college, Mr. Washington rode horse-drawn carriages, when he was lucky, and *walked* almost 500 miles! Can you imagine? But he went to school! And he didn't stop with earning a college degree for himself. He also founded a college for others. That college—Tuskegee Institute—is still here today. Remember, with faith and hard work all things are possible! You must never give up!" When Fia thought about her principal's speech, she felt better.

But then she thought about four little girls in Birmingham, Alabama who went to church one Sunday morning and who never came back home—four little girls—killed by a bomb in Sunday school. Fia felt sad again. "Were they fighting a losing battle?" she asked herself.

Fia sat very still, lost in her thoughts, her shoulders rounded with the weight of her questions. Then the cloud began to move again. "Where are we going now, Nana Bea?" Fia asked.

"To a very special place, Fia," Nana Bea responded.

As quickly as you could blink your eyes, Fia and Nana Bea were looking down at a small group of school-like buildings that seemed to glow in the light of the afternoon sun. Hanging to dry on clotheslines were brightly colored clothes, unfurling like sails in the gentle Kenyan breeze. The air was filled with the glorious harmonies of marvelous voices—children's voices joined in song. The rich sounds filled Fia's heart with joy. Fia looked at Nana Bea and saw that her wings were shimmering brightly. "Where are we, Nana Bea?" Fia asked.

"Down there is the Wema Centre for Children," Nana Bea said.

"The Wema Centre? What's that?"

"The Wema Centre is a home for children who had no homes but the streets. But now these children have a new chance at life." Nana Bea and Fia looked down. The children—most of them girls—were sitting in a circle beneath a large tree.

"Look over there," said Fia. "There's one girl standing all alone. I wonder why."

"That girl is upset," Nana Bea told Fia. "Today at school a teacher accused her of throwing paper across the room."

" 'I didn't do it!' the girl shouted angrily, knocking her desk over and running out of the room. Actually, the girl was telling the truth. But she made a big mistake. She told the truth in the wrong way. She was rude and disrespectful. And so she got into big trouble—not only with the teacher but also with the headmaster of the school," Nana Bea explained.

"Oh! Here comes one of the older girls. She's going to bring her into the circle with the others," said Fia. "I'm glad." The girl joined the group but she sat with her head down, her brow furrowed, and her arms folded tightly across her body. "I know just how she feels," Fia thought.

Nana Bea whispered into Fia's ear, "A storyteller from the United States of America is here to visit. Let's listen."

Before the visitor began, the children of the Wema Centre told their story in words and songs. "We were on the streets," the children said. "We had been thrown away like trash. Nobody cared for us and we didn't care for ourselves. When night came, we slept in the back roads of the town. Every night when we went to sleep, we wondered if we would wake to see another day. And some of us didn't care. 'What good will another day hold for us?' we asked. But then we came to the Wema Centre," they said joyously. "Here, with the help of God and good teachers, our lives have changed. Now we have hope. We have hope for ourselves. We have hope for each other. We have hope for the world!" Then the children sang songs of joyous praise. They sang in harmony, their voices blending together into one awesome sound. It was beautiful!

Next, a man introduced the storyteller from the United States. "A very long time ago," the man began, "some of our people were stolen away from our African Motherland. They were taken to a distant land and forced into slavery—forced to work without pay for others. Meet a great-great grandchild of those stolen people. Welcome her and listen to her stories."

"Thank you," said the storyteller in English. "*Asante sana*," she repeated in *Kiswahili*. The woman was tall, with a long graceful neck and full lips that stretched into the warmest smile Fia had ever seen.

Fia gave a little gasp. "That woman looks kind of familiar, Nana Bea. Do I know her?"

Nana Bea smiled. "You will know her one day, Fia," she said. "Now, listen!"

The storyteller walked in a circle among the children. "It's true," she said. "Many years ago, our people were taken into slavery. They were made to work for others. They were victims of hideous cruelty. But after all of those terrible times—look!—I am here. My presence tells you that some of your ancestors survived those terrible times. They survived because they had faith. They survived because they were strong. And they survived because they had dreams—dreams of a better future for their children and for their children's children.

"There is a river," the storyteller continued. "There is a river of the present that contains our own lives. There is a river of the future that contains the lives of our children. And there is a river of the past that contains the lives of our ancestors. I am here with you today because of those ancestors. I am here with you today because of people who entered the freedom river of our history, and who moved it forward—people like Harriet Tubman, Sojourner Truth, Frederick Douglass, Benjamin Banneker, Lewis Latimer, Booker T. Washington, W.E.B. Du Bois, Mary McCleod Bethune, George Washington Carver, Marcus Mosiah Garvey, and Charles Richard Drew . . . people like Rosa Parks, Martin Luther King, Jr., Medgar Evers, Fannie Lou Hamer, and Malcolm X . . . orators, writers, mathematicians, educators, institution builders, publishers, botanists, researchers, and freedom fighters who sacrificed their energy, their blood, and their very lives in the struggle to improve the world.

"I'm going to sing a song for you," the storyteller continued, "a song from that river of freedom, a song from our people in the United States, a song from our struggle." The storyteller began to sing:

Ain't gonna let nobody turn me 'round
Turn me 'round, turn me 'round!
Ain't gonna let nobody turn me 'round!
I'm going to keep on talking, keep on marching!
Marching on to freedom land!

The storyteller sang the song again and again and the

children and their teachers sang with her. Soon, everyone was singing, *Ain't gonna let nobody turn me 'round!*

Then the storyteller got the spirit. Her voice sounded strong and deep as she told the children, "Don't you let anybody turn you around! March on to your freedom land!

"There will be trials," she said. "You know about trials. There will be hardships. You know about hardships, too. But you can rise above the trials and you can rise above the hardships. You can survive and you can thrive. You can march on to your freedom land! That is the message I bring to you from the freedom river—the river of our African ancestors."

The children leaned forward, their eyes following the storyteller, their hearts opening to her words. "Now I will tell you a true story about a man I will call Mr. Joe, one of the ancestors from that freedom river. Mr. Joe was an enslaved African, a black man who lived through the slavery times in the United States of America. Listen to Mr. Joe's story."

Mr. Joe's Story

> One day, Mr. Joe was sitting on his front porch with a little girl 8 or 9 years old. Mr. Joe was rocking back and forth in his rocking chair and the little girl was sitting on the steps at his feet. They were listening to the birds. They often sat like this, the little girl and Mr. Joe. Usually, they sat in silence. Sometimes Mr. Joe would name the birds that were singing. He knew the names of all the birds even though he couldn't see them. Mr. Joe was blind. He had ugly scars on his face where his eyes should have been. Mr. Joe and his young friend never talked about those scars. They didn't talk about the slavery times either. But this day was different. Mr. Joe decided to

tell his story. "If they ever brought back the slavery times, I would just as soon lie down and die," Mr. Joe said. "They didn't treat a slave no better than you would treat a dog."

Then the little girl asked, "Mr. Joe, how come you're blind? Does it have something to do with slavery?"

"I'll tell you," Mr. Joe responded. He was quiet for a long time and then he said again, "I'll tell you." Finally, he said: "When I was a little tyke, just about your age, I used to like to sit up under the bridge and try to scratch out letters and words in the mud. But one day, the overseer caught me. He called everybody together and he told us—'Now, you all know it's illegal for a slave to try to learn to read and write. I'm gonna teach this boy a lesson and I want it to be a lesson to all of you.' While he was talking, he was taking out his whip. Then he tied me down. I squeezed my eyes shut to stop the tears. I knew what was coming next.

"WHOP! WHOP! WHOP! The whip came down on my back and then on my legs, on my arms, and on my face! Again and again the whip tore into my body. That overseer beat me bad. And he made everybody watch. Couldn't nobody come and help me, *nobody*—not even my mama. And then, when I thought the beating couldn't get any worse, when I felt like I was surely gonna die, that ol' overseer reached down. He reached down and took a hot, burning stick off the fire and—and he burned out my eyes. He burned out my eyes 'cause I was trying to learn to read and write."

Mr. Joe stopped talking for a long time. He didn't move. The little girl sat still, too. Finally, Mr. Joe said, "That's why I always tell you to get your education, child. Get your education. I couldn't, but you can." Mr. Joe shook his head. "I couldn't, but you can."

Everyone was very quiet. Then the storyteller said, "There is a river of people like Mr. Joe—people who had the fortitude to survive, the courage to resist, and the faith to struggle in order to make things better for the children, in order to make things better for those coming on. There is a river of people with the determination and the commitment to continue the struggle for freedom. Become a part of that river," the storyteller said, looking into the eyes of each child.

"Remember, children, education is the key that unlocks the golden door to freedom. Get a good education so you can take care of yourself. And then give something back to your family, to your community, and to your Creator." As the storyteller spoke, the angry girl—who had been sitting with her head lowered—raised her head, relaxed her face, and unfolded her arms.

Then the storyteller said, "Now I will tell you another story about the importance of education. This is my own version of one of *Aesop's Fables*. In this story, called 'The Lion and the Mouse,' you will meet a teacher who uses her own lesson to save her life. In my version of this story, the mouse is a schoolteacher," the storyteller said. "Imagine that—a mouse teaching school!" All of the children smiled. Fia smiled too, as the storyteller began.

The Lion and the Mouse

Ms. Mouse was feeling quite wonderful! Her day at school had been very full and the day had gone quite well. In honor of Black History Month, Ms. Mouse had taught her students about Mr. Booker T. Washington, the black leader who was born into slavery in the United States. Mr. Washington was an amazing person who lifted himself up from slavery to get an education for himself and then founded a college so that others could get an education, too.

"I am sure my students got the message—education is the key to progress. With faith and education, truly all things are possible!" said the dedicated little teacher as she scurried through the forest. She was feeling on top of the world.

But then, Ms. Mouse bumped into Mr. Lion.

Mr. Lion was pacing back and forth roaring, "I'm hungry! I'm hungry!" When Mr. Lion looked down and saw Ms. Mouse, he picked her up by the tail and prepared to drop her into his mouth. "Oh, Mr. Lion, Mr. Lion, please don't eat me! I'm too small! Eating me would be like eating just one potato chip!"

"It's true, Ms. Mouse, you are mighty small, but even one little chip is better than nothing at all," Mr. Lion replied with a deafening roar.

Ms. Mouse knew she had to think fast. And then it came to her! She remembered the lesson she taught her students about Mr. Booker T. Washington who said:

When your head is in the lion's mouth,
You'd best use your hands to stroke his mane.

"Mr. Lion," Ms. Mouse cajoled. "You are truly a noble being, the king of all the animals. A great animal like you deserves a banquet, not a small meal like me. Please, Mr. Lion, show how wonderful you are and let me go."

The flattery worked! Mr. Lion smiled. He thought, "Mouse is right. Eating something so small would only make me hungrier." So Mr. Lion let Ms. Mouse go.

"Oh, thank you so much for your generosity, Mr. Lion!" Ms. Mouse exclaimed. "One good turn deserves another. Perhaps I can help you someday."

"You help me?" Mr. Lion replied, roaring with laughter. "Now that's a good one! Well now, Ms. Mouse, you didn't provide a meal but you were good for a laugh, and laughter is food for the soul! HA! HA! HA!" laughed Mr. Lion as he lumbered off to continue his search for food.

Now some of you already know what happened. The very next day, Mr. Lion was trapped by the ropes of a hunter. Roaring with pain, Mr.

Lion pulled at the ropes, trying to free himself. But the more he pulled the tighter the ropes became. His strength did not help him. Mr. Lion was sure that he was done for.

But tiny Ms. Mouse heard Mr. Lion's roars. She responded immediately! With her sharp teeth, Ms. Mouse nibbled quickly through the ropes and freed Mr. Lion from the trap. "Thank you, Ms. Mouse," Mr. Lion said humbly. "I have learned an important lesson. You don't have to be big in order to make a difference!"

"Step on a tin, the tin bends. That's the way my story ends," the storyteller said. The children and their teachers applauded enthusiastically. The storyteller bowed and smiled happily.

Then the school's counselor stood up. "Thank you very much," he said to the storyteller. "We are richer because we have heard your stories. You told us about our ancestors who were stolen away from our African Motherland. We will always remember this history. We will never forget the sacrifices our ancestors made for us," the counselor said solemnly.

"Then you told us about Mr. Joe, who was blinded because he wanted to learn to read and write. Mr. Joe's story reminds us that education is a privilege. We will always remember Mr. Joe. We will always remember the value of a good education."

The counselor looked at the girl who had been so angry. "Your last story contains another important lesson," he said. "When your head is in the lion's mouth, use your hands to massage his mane. As the counselor spoke, the girl smiled and nodded her head in agreement.

The counselor smiled, too, and addressed the group. "Sometimes we can be right, but we turn our right into a wrong when we shout and misbehave. Stroking the mane of the lion means to control your anger. It means to always treat others with respect. Then you can fulfill your purpose in life. Then you can move toward your own best future."

The counselor turned to the storyteller. "Thank you for these lessons."

"Thank you for listening," the storyteller replied.

"Oh, thank you for bringing me here, Nana Bea," said Fia. "I'll never forget it. What *Kwanzaa* word do you want me to remember?" she asked.

"The word is *Nia*," Nana Bea responded. "*Nia* means purpose. Do you see the connection, Fia?"

"I think I do," said Fia. "I think we have to remember our purpose in life—to get a good education so we can . . ." Fia stopped talking in the middle of her sentence. She heard the children of the Wema Centre singing *Ain't gonna let nobody turn me 'round!* Fia rocked from side to side, enchanted by their beautiful voices. Then, to Fia's surprise, the Wema Centre children changed the words to the song.

She leaned forward, listening carefully. Then she smiled and sang along with the other children, singing wonderful new words to the old melody.

I'm going to go to school and make A's and B's,
A's and B's, A's and B's!
I'm going to go to school and make A's and B's!
I'm going to keep on learning, keep on striving!
I know that education is the key!

"What a great song!" Fia said joyously, continuing to sing as she and Nana Bea floated away on their cloud, high above the majestic Kenyan countryside.

Questions for Readers from **The Purpose Story**

Discuss the questions below.
Write your responses to each question in two or three sentences.

1. What does the word *courageous* mean? In what two or three ways were the people in the Civil Rights Movement courageous?

2. What did Fia's principal tell his students in order to encourage them? What three experiences from the life of Mr. Booker T. Washington did he use as examples? What quotation from Mr. Washington did all of the students at Fia's school say in unison at the assembly? What does this quotation mean to you?

3. At the beginning of the story, Fia's shoulders are "rounded with the weight of her questions." What are Fia's questions? What two or three questions do you have about life?

4. **The Purpose Story** is named "History Lessons from a Storyteller." If you had to give this story another name, what would you name it?

5. How many history lessons can you find in **The Purpose Story**? What lesson is first? What lessons come after that? What lesson comes last?

6. Why was Mr. Joe blinded in "Mr. Joe's Story?" What lesson will you always remember from "Mr. Joe's Story?"

7. In what two or three ways can you compare and contrast "Mr. Joe's Story" with "The Lion and the Mouse?"

8. Think about the angry girl in the story. How do you think the angry girl *should* have responded when she was falsely accused? Rewrite the scene to reflect your opinion.

9. Describe a situation—real or imagined—that is similar to that of the angry girl in **The Purpose Story**. What advice would you give to the angry girl or boy in the situation you described?

10. How can learning history help us to improve our lives? Make a chart listing and briefly describing each history lesson in **The Purpose Story**. Next to each lesson, write what that history lesson teaches you about what you can do to lead a better life today.

11. What two or three lessons did Fia learn in **The Purpose Story?**

12. What is the most important lesson for *you* in **The Purpose Story**? Why?

Character Development Activities For THE PURPOSE STORY

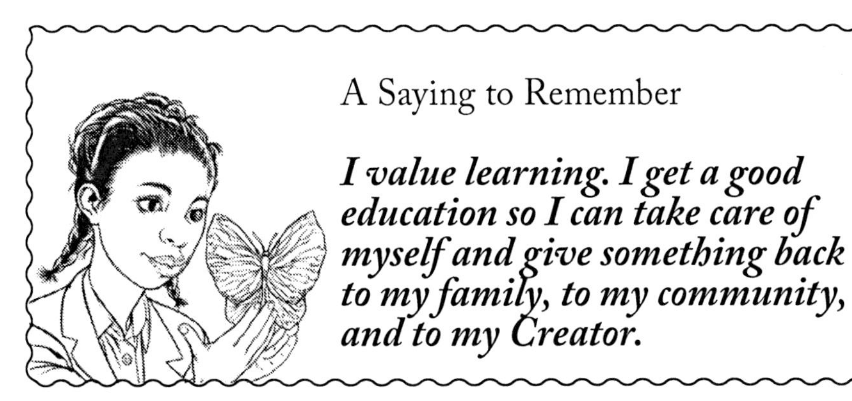

1. Copy the saying to remember for **The Purpose Story**. Put the saying in a special place.

2. Memorize the saying and think about what it means to you.

3. Write a 5- to 8-sentence paragraph that describes how you relate the saying to your own life. Include the following in your paragraph:

    a. What this saying means to you

    b. How you will use this saying to improve yourself in one or more of the following areas: your health, your schoolwork, your attitude, your thoughts and feelings about yourself, your relationships with others, and/or your daily behavior

    Share your paragraph with an encouraging friend or with a supportive adult.

4. Make a list of real-world tasks that you can undertake in order to make the lessons you learned in **The Purpose Story** a reality in your life. See the starter list below for ideas.

    a. Aim to go to school and to every class every day. Aim to be on time every day!
    b. Always do your homework and turn it in on time. Follow directions and be thorough. Make your homework assignments neat and complete!
    c. Read three to five extra books each month. Write reviews of the books you read.
    d. Make a list of African-American heroes and heroines. Write two or three accomplishments and/or admirable qualities next to the name of each person on your list. Highlight three to five of the qualities and/or accomplishments that are special to you. Write these qualities and/or accomplishments next to your own name.
    e. Find one of *Aesop's Fables* in a storybook or on the Internet. Use your imagination to rewrite the fable to make a point about the value of education.

5. Take action on the real-world tasks on your list. Record your experiences in a special journal.

Character Development Reminder

***Think about it!* Since a good education is your key to a successful future, you should make paying attention, respecting your teachers, and following school rules as natural as breathing. Remember, education is a privilege.**

A Saying to Remember for
The Creativity Story

I cultivate joy, laughter, and hope. I activate my artistry in my own special way.

Fia and the Butterfly: 7 Stories for Character Education
Dr. Lonnetta M. Taylor-Gaines

The Creativity Story

Fia Makes the Sun Shine

Setting: Wasini Island, Kenya, East Africa

Fia shifted a little on their cloud, first one way and then another. When she shifted again, Nana Bea said, "Fia, you seem fidgety. What's on your mind? What are you wishing for right now?"

"Nana Bea, floating over the country of Kenya on this cloud is wonderful—it's like being in a dream. But I wish I could go down there and see what's on the ground, I mean see everything up close."

"That's possible, Fia."

"It is? How can I get down there, Nana Bea?"

Nana Bea responded, "You already know that you can travel on the wings of your wishes. That's how you got here. But do you know that you can also travel through the power of your memory?"

Fia shook her head. "That sounds weird, Nana Bea."

"I'll show you, Fia. What's your very favorite memory?"

Fia answered immediately, hugging her knees and rocking back and forth as she talked: "My favorite memory is being on the beach in Mobile with my mother, my Aunt Omelia, and my cousin Claudine. We walked out onto the jetty which was like a wooden sidewalk on long legs over the water. At the end of the jetty there was a little house—well, more like a porch than a house with a slanting roof but no walls, only rails so you wouldn't fall in. We took heavy string and tied fat meat to the end. We lowered the meat into the water and waited to feel a tug. Then we eased the string up—slowly, slowly—until we saw a crab nibbling at the fat meat. Then—ever so carefully—we took a net with a long handle and scooped the crab up and dumped it into our bucket. It was so much fun! After our bucket was full of crabs, we walked back up the jetty to the beach house and my mother and my Aunt Omelia cooked the crabs. It was the best! I just love crabs!"

"Then I know just the place for you, Fia. Here in Kenya there is a place called Wasini Island. I think you'll find something there that you like to eat," said Nana Bea. "And when you come back, Fia, it will be your turn to be the storyteller." Then, in a velvety-soft voice, Nana Bea said, "Now, Fia, be quiet and be still. Let your body relax. Feel your memory, see your memory, be your memory." As Fia listened to Nana Bea, she began to feel very peaceful. Then Fia floated downward—like a feather on the wind—until she landed lightly on the welcoming earth. Nana Bea folded her wings and waited patiently for Fia to return.

When Fia came back, Nana Bea whispered—so softly that Fia could barely hear her—"Activate your artistry, Fia. Tell your story." Then, in a normal voice, Nana Bea asked Fia, "Did you have a nice time?"

"Oh, Nana Bea, it was wonderful! It was just wonderful!" Fia said.

"What did you do, Fia?" Nana Bea asked.

"I was with a group of tourists. We took a ride on a long narrow boat called a *dhow* to the place you told me about. We went to Wasini Island."

"And the weather, Fia?"

"It was raining, raining, and raining, Nana Bea! It didn't look like the sun would ever shine again! Some people were chilly but not me! I wasn't cold at all. My school uniform kept me warm. Then guess what happened! I made the sun shine! I made the sun shine, Nana Bea!" Fia repeated.

Nana Bea smiled broadly, "Fia, I think you are ready to tell your story!"

Fia lay on her stomach and stretched over the edge of the cloud to get a last look at Wasini Island. She looked sad. "It was so good and now it's over," Fia moaned.

"It's not over, Fia. As long as you tell the story, you will remember," Nana Bea said. "Tell your story, Fia."

Fia smiled and began: "It happened like this. It was July—wintertime in Kenya, East Africa—and Sun was taking a much-needed rest. During most of the year, Sun works very hard in Kenya, shining brightly and bringing a tremendous amount of heat to the land. July was vacation time for Sun. 'Let the clouds do some work. Today I intend to rest,' Sun said that morning, and Sun meant it.

"Later in the day, one of the clouds passed by the room where Sun was resting. Now all of the clouds knew that no one was allowed to disturb Sun during rest time. But this cloud had something to say and her name wasn't Bold Cloud for nothing. 'Nothing ventured, nothing gained,' Bold Cloud thought as she floated over to Sun's room and tapped gently on the door. Sun called out gruffly, 'Come in.'

"Bold Cloud floated slowly into Sun's room. 'Bold Cloud, this had better be important!' Sun grunted.

" 'Oh, it is,' said Bold Cloud. 'I just saw a boat full of

tourists taking a cruise to Wasini Island.'

" 'So, what else is new?' asked Sun, saying each word very slowly in a scorching voice that would have frightened most clouds. 'Tourists are a part of life here in Kenya. I'm glad they're here, but I don't understand why you have interrupted my sleep to tell me about them.'

" 'Well,' Bold Cloud said, 'the tourists are quite chilly because of the rain. If you would only come out of your room, those tourists would be warm in a minute!'

" 'Humph,' replied Sun. 'Why are you bothering me, you busybody cloud? This is my vacation and I will not be disturbed!' Sun said it and Sun meant it! And that was that!

"Now not every cloud was brave enough to speak directly to Sun. That Bold Cloud was a risk taker. And Bold Cloud didn't give up just because Sun told her 'no.' To Bold Cloud, the word 'no' meant come up with another idea. A polite request had not worked. 'But there is more than one way to make the sun shine,' Bold Cloud whispered to herself. 'I just need to think.' "

"**Bold Cloud floated** down closer to Wasini Island. There she saw the tiny wild goats scampering about. Their kids were pretending that they were mountain goats climbing on the island's gently sloping paths. 'Nehhehey! Nehhehey!' the goats called cheerfully to Bold Cloud. Bold Cloud was always glad to see the frisky goats. She smiled and waved at them, but she didn't stop to talk–not today. Bold Cloud was thinking.

"Bold Cloud continued to float over Wasini Island. She floated over the school where the island children were in the middle of their English lesson. She floated over a village weaver who sat in a trench in the earth making brightly colored scarves from silken threads. She floated over the Wasini Island Restaurant where the tourists were enjoying their lunch. Bold Cloud stopped suddenly. She had an idea!

"Bold Cloud knew just what to do to get Sun to shine. She laughed gleefully as she looked down at the Wasini Island Restaurant where the tourists were feasting on the giant island crabs. Did I say feasting? Those tourists were eating those crabs like there was no tomorrow! Crack! Went the heavy wooden knives against the claws of the freshly steamed crabs, and whoosh went the shells as they flew high into the air releasing the white crabmeat. The tourists ate with joyful gusto. No one seemed to notice the empty crab shells piling up around them like small mountains. Those tourists kept right on eating!

"Bold Cloud turned to another cloud floating beside her. 'What do you think of that?'

" 'It's amazing! I've never seen anyone eat like that!' the other cloud replied. 'What do you think we should do, Bold Cloud?'

"Bold Cloud smiled. This was working out just as she had planned. 'I think we should tell the others to come look!' she said. 'Surely, this is something worth talking about!'

" 'You're right, Bold Cloud!' her friend replied happily and went floating across the sky to help spread the word about the tourists with the humongous appetites. Clouds just love to talk, you know, so soon all of the clouds were chattering noisily about the Crab Feast at Wasini Island. Bold Cloud's plan was working!

"Now Sun—who was far too curious to stay inside with all of this chattering going on—rolled out of his gigantic bed and peeked through his door to see what was happening. 'Ohhh!' said the tourists, smiling with delight as they looked at the rainbow that Sun made as his rays shone through the rain. Then Sun shone brightly and the rain stopped.

"The clouds were delighted! 'Bold Cloud, you did it! Your plan worked!' they exclaimed. 'Where there's a will, there's a way,' they chanted happily. 'Sun came out on a rainy day! Where there's a will, there has to be a way! Sun came out on a rainy day!' "

Fia ended her story with a smile of satisfaction.

"**That's a lovely** story, Fia," Nana Bea said. "But where do you come in?"

"Nana Bea," Fia replied happily, "I'm the one who gave Bold Cloud her idea. I ate a *ton* of crabs! When Bold Cloud saw how many steamed crabs *I* was eating, she knew the clouds would talk, and she knew that Sun would hear the chattering and come outside. So you see," Fia concluded with a flourish, "it was me who made the sun shine that rainy day on Wasini Island—of course, with the help of a risk-taking cloud! How's *that* for a story?"

"Well done, Fia!" Nana Bea exclaimed enthusiastically, fluttering her wings with pleasure. "You've got *Kuumba*!"

"I've got what, Nana Bea?"

"You've got *Kuumba*, creativity, the sixth principle," said Nana Bea. "Use your *Kuumba* to cultivate joy, laughter, and hope. Use your *Kuumba* to activate your artistry in your own special way. Joy, laughter, hope, artistry—those are the lifesavers, Fia, and *Kuumba* is the key."

"I've got *Kuumba*!" Fia laughed and laughed. "Hey! I've got *KUUMBA*!"

Questions for Readers from **The Creativity Story**

Discuss the questions below.
Write your responses to each question in two or three sentences.

1. What does the word *fidgety* mean? Why was Fia fidgety on the cloud?

2. What is Fia's favorite memory? Give at least three details. What is your favorite personal memory? Give at least three details.

3. What does Nana Bea say to help Fia float down to earth?

4. **The Creativity Story** is named "Fia Makes the Sun Shine." If you had to give this story another name, what would you name it?

5. What does Bold Cloud do first to try to get Sun to shine? When that doesn't work, what does she do next? What does she finally do?

6. Why do the tourists see a rainbow when Sun begins to shine?

7. In what two or three ways are you similar to Bold Cloud? In what two or three ways are you different from Bold Cloud?

8. What parts of this story do you think are silly or humorous? Why?

9. In your opinion, what's the best food in the whole world? Write a paragraph about a time when you ate and enjoyed your favorite food.

10. How do you think Fia turned her love for her favorite food into a creative story? Write, draw, or paste a picture of your favorite food in the center of a plain sheet of paper. Now use your imagination to brainstorm words and unusual or funny ideas about what happens when you or someone else eats your favorite food. Use your ideas to write a silly or humorous story about your favorite food.

11. What two or three lessons did Fia learn in **The Creativity Story**?

12. What is the most important lesson for *you* in **The Creativity Story**? Why?

Character Development Activities For THE CREATIVITY STORY

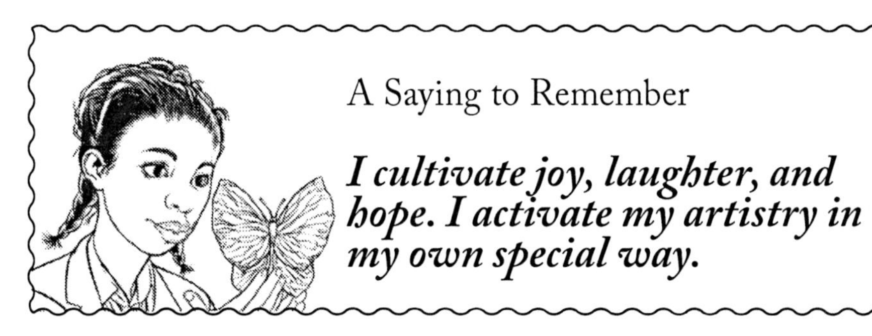

A Saying to Remember

I cultivate joy, laughter, and hope. I activate my artistry in my own special way.

1. Copy the saying to remember for **The Creativity Story.** Put the saying in a special place.

2. Memorize the saying and think about what it means to you.

3. Write a 5- to 8-sentence paragraph that describes how you relate the saying to your own life. Include the following in your paragraph:

   a. What this saying means to you

   b. How you will use this saying to improve yourself in one or more of the following areas: your health, your schoolwork, your attitude, your thoughts and feelings about yourself, your relationships with others, and/or your daily behavior

Share your paragraph with an encouraging friend or with a supportive adult.

4. Make a list of real-world tasks that you can undertake in order to make the lessons you learned in **The Creativity Story** a reality in your life. See the starter list below for ideas.

   a. Make a list of your special artistic gifts. Take classes at school or elsewhere to cultivate those gifts.
   b. Look at arts programs on public television and other TV channels.
   c. Find and listen to radio stations that feature classic jazz and other forms of classical music. Listen to classical music at least one hour per week.
   d. Try to make your room or personal space at home a work of art. Keep your space orderly and add decorations that express your personality.
   e. Write about your experiences and memories. Turn some of your experiences and memories into creative stories. Share your stories with others.

5. Take action on the real-world tasks on your list. Record your experiences in a special journal.

Character Development Reminder

Think about it! **You don't have to be an artist to appreciate the arts. Visit museums and go to dance performances, plays, and concerts. Remember—the arts can enrich your life and expand your world.**

A Saying to Remember for
The Faith Story

I practice faith in action.
I am moving forward
to meet my good

Fia and the Butterfly: 7 Stories for Character Education
Dr. Lonnetta M. Taylor-Gaines

The Faith Story

How Butterflies Came to Be

Setting: The Mwaluganje Elephant Sanctuary, Kwale District, Kenya

"N**ana Bea," Fia** lamented, "I almost don't want to hear the seventh story because it's the last one."

"Yes, Fia, but it's time for you to hear this last story. And that means our time together is coming to an end. And that's all right, Fia."

"It's not all right, Nana Bea," Fia said, beginning to cry. "I'll miss you, Nana, I'll miss you!"

"Fia, I know," Nana Bea said tenderly. "I know there is something in your life that is making you feel afraid."

"You're right, Nana Bea. I have been scared recently," Fia said softly.

"Tell me, Fia, what is it?"

"I haven't told anybody," Fia said reluctantly, "not even my mother, and I tell my mother everything."

"I know, Fia," Nana Bea prodded. "Go on."

"Well, Nana," Fia said in a rush, "I'm afraid to go to church!"

"Why, Fia?"

"Nana Bea, my grandmother lives in Birmingham, Alabama. I love visiting her every summer and walking up the hills in the sunshine to go to Sunday School and church. It's so pretty!"

"Yes, Fia, go on."

"But, Nana Bea, just two months ago, on Sunday, September 15, 1963—I'll never forget that date—right there in Birmingham where my grandmother lives, bad people bombed a church and killed four little girls. They murdered them in Sunday School, Nana Bea. One of the girls was 11 years old, just like me. I've been afraid ever since the bombing. I'm scared, Nana Bea, I'm scared."

"Okay, Fia, you have taken a very important step. You're bringing your fears out into the open. Now, Fia, you are ready to learn the seventh principle, which is *Imani. Imani* means faith. Nana Bea quoted: " '*Now faith is the substance of things hoped for, the evidence of things not seen.*' When you have faith, Fia, you can live . . . "

Fia interrupted Nana Bea. "Faith? Faith didn't save those four little girls, Nana Bea. How can faith help?"

"Fia, faith isn't something that you practice just when things are going well," Nana Bea said, brushing Fia's arm gently with a fluttering wing. "Faith is most helpful during the hard times, when things seem to be at their worst."

Fia moved restlessly on the cloud. "But Nana Bea . . ."

"Hear me out, Fia," said Nana Bea. "I know this is a hard lesson to learn. That's why *Imani*—faith—is the seventh principle." Nana Bea sighed and looked closely at Fia. "I hope you can learn from this, my last story. It's a story from the beginnings of the world. It's the story of how butterflies came to be."

Fia settled down, and Nana Bea began her story.

"**Long ago when t**he earth was new, there were no animals in the world—there were no elephants, no giraffes, no impalas, no cheetahs, no gazelles, no lions, no ostriches, and no zebras. There was not even a bug, not a beetle, not a spider, no, not even a mosquito. This was the time before butterflies. Can you imagine that?" With a contented smile, Fia closed her eyes and snuggled close. Nana Bea continued, "Now, think a moment. Even though there were no creatures in the world, there was still life.

"There was fertile Earth, rich and dark and beautiful. On Earth, there were towering mountains and endless valleys. There were the trees, flowers, grasses, and shrubs. There were the life-giving waters, far-reaching seas, endless oceans, winding rivers, sparkling lakes, rapidly rushing streams, and tiny trickling brooks. It was magnificent!

"Above Earth stretched vast reaches of Sky with cottony clouds, brightly twinkling stars, and the ephemeral moon. Of course, there was the majestic sun, shining forth mightily in Sky's infinite embrace. Yes, there was life.

"Life, with its ongoing cycles giving rhythm to the world—the heat of the sun changing Earth's moisture into mist, mist rising upward to Sky to make the clouds, the clouds themselves transforming and returning once more to Earth as rain or fog or snow or freezing sleet.

"And at the center of it all was the Spirit of the Wind, blowing soft and fierce, warm and cold, mixing the elements until Earth came forth with her bounty: strong, solid trees with leafy branches reaching upward, willowy rushes bending under the gentle pressure of the morning rain, and lovely flowers—an honor guard of colors—joyously proclaiming the Spirit of Life. It was beautiful."

"**But then, right** when it seemed as if everything was running smoothly, along came a big crisis. It all started when

Earth and Sky fell in love."

Fia giggled gleefully.

"Oh, yes!" Nana Bea continued. "There's nothing like love to stir things up and that's a fact! That's why love is for when you already know who you are as a person and have something to give to a relationship. Oh, yes! But that's another story. Now where was I?" Nana Bea asked. "Oh!" she said with a smile as she remembered.

"So Earth and Sky fell in love—how could they help it? They spent all of their time looking at each other. In fact, all they could see was each other. Earth would look up at Sky in utter amazement. At night she saw the clouds wafting by, the stars sparkling, and the moon glowing, only to be replaced by the powerful presence of the sun at daybreak. Earth saw these things, and she fell in love with Sky's magnificence.

"Sky also loved Earth. Looking down, he saw Earth's lush richness. Sky loved the many colors of Earth and never tired of watching the rhythm of Earth's cyclic changes. But this love was not a simple love—what love is? Although Earth loved Sky, she was also overwhelmed by Sky's power. She saw the great huge light of the sun, the bright-glittering stars, and the evanescent glow of the moon, and she began to worry. Earth thought, 'I can never be as full of light as Sky. How can I believe that Sky could ever truly love me?'

"And Sky looked down on Earth and he, too, was distressed. Sky was in awe of Earth's rich, dark beauty and of her ability to create, to give birth again and again and again to mountains, to rivers, to trees, to plants, and to all flowering things. 'How can I ever know Earth's mysteries?' Sky wondered.

"The biggest problem Earth and Sky had was the distance between them. They just could not communicate. They tried to overcome it. The flowers and trees and grasses of Earth danced playfully in the wind and when they did, Sky felt Earth's love stirring in his heart. In return, Sky would reach toward Earth with the long arms of the moon, and the little stars would twinkle Sky's love messages to quiet, listening Earth. Then Earth and Sky felt close to each other, but they were still far apart.

"When Earth and Sky couldn't communicate, they became afraid. When Earth was afraid, she erupted with tremendous quakes. Then her volcanic mountains overflowed with lava and her seas raged in great tidal waves. When Sky was fearful, he sent down chilling blizzards and tremendous thunderstorms followed by parching droughts fueled by the burning rays of the sun.

"Life during those times was terrible for the children of Earth. All of the plants were dying. Without water, the trees and the grasses and the flowers were drying up, shriveling, unable to get sustenance from parched Earth. Sky's children suffered, too. The stars and the moon and the clouds stared mournfully at the destruction below.

"And then, one terrible day, the moon moved in front of the sun and all of a sudden, day became night—oh my Lord!—and there shuddering in the darkness, the children of Earth and the children of Sky knew that something had to change."

"**And so the** children of Sky—the clouds, the stars, and the moon—and the children of Earth—the trees, the flowers, the shrubs, and the grasses—came together. Even the distant sun decided to join them. It was just that serious! They all gathered in the valley of the baobab trees between the two highest mountain peaks on Earth. They chose this place because the mountains were where Earth jutted upward to Sky and where the clouds hovered downward, swirling around the trees and the grassy hilltops as if Sky were lowering itself down to earth. They also wanted to be in the presence of the wise old baobab trees. They needed help!

"Of course, the Spirit of the Wind was also there with them, watching and waiting to see what they would do.

"An elder baobab called everyone to order and then the bickering began. One of the oak trees said, 'Our main problem is to figure out what to do about that finicky Sky. What with these ice storms one day and burning heat the next, my leaves are just plain confused. They start turning red and gold thinking winter is coming and it's time for them to fall. Then the weather changes and they start clinging again.'

" 'I resent that,' said Moon. 'I don't know how you can blame Sky for a problem with your stupid little leaves. The real problem is Earth. That last volcano had the clouds so scared they didn't know what to do—rain, snow, sleet, or hail. Earth just needs to calm down.'

" 'Now wait a minute, Miz Moon,' shouted one of the shrubs. 'You're the one that caused that tidal wave that completely destroyed all of our relatives down South. And furthermore . . .'

" 'Now you just need to shut up, you little shrub,' Moon retorted. 'You can't blame me for that tidal wave. I'm just up here minding my own sweet business.'

" 'Yeah, and just what business is that, I want to know,' said one of the willow trees.

" 'Oh, let's all listen now,' said one of the stars. 'Miss Weeping Willow has a comment. Just what does the crybaby have to say?'

" 'I'm not a crybaby,' the willow wailed.

" 'Now, see what you've done, you ol' ice-cold, unfeeling star!' said a group of flowers who rushed over to comfort the willow tree. 'All of you stars are just plain heartless— no feelings at all. That's the problem.'

" 'Oh, hush your mouths,' bellowed one of the storm clouds. 'Who cares about you namby-pamby little flowers anyway? I can send down some lightning and settle all of this right now.'

" 'That's exactly what we're talking about,' all the plants yelled. 'Your warmongering is what got us into this fix in the first place.'

"Back and forth they went, the children of Earth blaming Sky for the crisis and the children of Sky blaming Earth. Their bickering became louder and louder until—quite suddenly—the Spirit of the Wind moved rapidly through the branches of the gigantic baobab trees, making an awesome sound and scaring both the Earth and Sky children into a petrified silence."

"Finally, Wind became still and it was absolutely quiet. Then the eldest baobab spoke to the gathering. 'We all agree that we have a problem,' the baobab said. 'Now let's make the decision to solve our problem. Getting here wasn't easy, but you managed it. The larger trees helped the small saplings. The clouds provided shade for the weary flowers. At night, the moon and the stars lit the way. In order to get here, you accepted responsibility for each other. Now let's accept responsibility for solving our own problems and stop blaming either Earth or Sky. I challenge you—let's solve our problems for ourselves.'

"Well! Everyone was stunned. They sat there in silence for quite some time. No one could answer the baobab's challenge. Finally, just when they were ready to give up, they heard a squeaky little voice. It was the thistle, the tiniest and most humble of the plants. The little thistle said, 'If we want to solve our problems, we must each give something of ourselves. Just talking will not help. I'm not large like some of you,' continued the thistle, 'but I will give what I have.' Then the thistle tossed one of its tiny leaves into the valley of the baobab. Everyone watched as the tiny leaf floated to the bottom of the valley. 'The smallest and most humble among us has pointed the way,' they said solemnly.

"As Sky's children and the children of Earth left the valley, they all gave up a part of themselves. Their gifts created a huge mound of multicolored bits in the valley of the baobab. There were deep-green blades of grass, red-orange leaves, rainbow-colored petals from all kinds of flowers, white-shimmering slivers of the moon, silvery sparkles from the twinkling stars, dark-colored bark from the trees, and misty-gray droplets from the clouds. There were even golden-bright pieces of the sun.

"The last to leave the valley that day was the beautiful purple *Bostani* plant. She had given so much of herself that she was feeling a little tired. She sat down to rest on the side of the mountain. And then she saw the miracle!"

"**The Spirit of** the Wind, moved by the offerings of the children of Earth and Sky, created a whirlwind in the valley, stirring the colorful mound into a fantastic multicolored spiral. Imagine! The colorful bits were swirling around and around, propelled by the Great Spirit. When finally Wind calmed down, the air was filled with newborn creatures flying with a life of their own.

"The new creatures were made from pieces of Sky and from pieces of Earth so they understood the language of both Earth and Sky. They were extraordinarily beautiful. The *Bostani* waved her lovely purple flowers in joyous gratitude. She knew that help had come. The newborn creatures hovered close to the purple plant, listening as she whispered, 'You are here to bring peace to our world. You are communicators. You are ambassadors of love.' Immediately, the new creatures began to fulfill their purpose, flying low and flying high, carrying messages between Earth and Sky.

"And so, Earth and Sky were able to live in harmony. All was well.

" 'What shall we call these amazing creatures?' everyone asked. 'Why, they are like *beauty flying,*' someone said. 'Let's call them that!' said one of the baobab trees. And so they did. The new creatures were called *beauty flying* for quite a while, but you know what happens with language. Everyone shortened *beauty flying* and began to call them beauty flies instead. Next, they changed *beauty flies,* so then everyone was calling the new creatures . . ."

"Butterflies!" Fia said with a big smile, bouncing about on the cloud. "I know! I know! It's like my Aunt Ora Lee's nickname. Everybody calls her *Muh Deah,* but we really mean *Mother Dear.* It's just that, well, Muh Deah just . . . it just slides on out!" Fia continued, "So I can understand how a *beauty fly* can become a *butterfly. Butterfly* just slides on out!"

"Yes, Fia," said Nana Bea, smiling. "And that's the end of the story. That's how butterflies came to be."

"**It's a beautiful** story, Nana Bea," said Fia. "I almost forgot that I was afraid. Is that the point, Nana Bea? Is that the lesson of faith?"

"No, Fia. It's the magic of creativity that makes you forget your fears. But stories lose their purpose if they make you forget completely. This butterfly story contains a message that will help you deal with the hard times. Can you figure it out, Fia?"

Fia took her time. She thought about the story again, from beginning to end, like a tape recording playing in her mind. Finally, speaking very slowly, Fia said: "I think the lesson is that even when things are horrible—as horrible as girls being killed in a church—we can still make things better. If everybody comes together and gives something of themselves—like Sky's children and the children of Earth did, like . . . like all those people who are marching together and fighting for freedom back home are doing—then something better has just got to happen."

"Fia," Nana Bea exclaimed, "you are like that tiny thistle in the story! You get right to the heart of the matter. I'm beginning to think that Fia not only stands for Fredericka Inez Anderson but also for faith in action."

"Faith in action—what does that mean, Nana Bea?"

"Acting as if you expect the best to happen, even when the going gets tough . . . moving forward to meet your good, even during the hard times—that's faith in action, Fia!"

"Faith in action," Fia repeated. "I like that, Nana Bea," Fia said with a little smile.

"Fia, I want you to remember that faith is something that you *do*. That is the lesson of the tiny thistle—you must act on your faith."

"Nana Bea," Fia murmured, "I still don't understand why those four little girls had to die."

"Fia, neither do I," Nana Bea admitted. "Death is a part of life, but some deaths stand out as a part of history. Sometimes when awful things happen, better things emerge. Look at the story of the butterflies. As a result of a crisis, beautiful new life emerged."

Nana Bea paused. Then she said: "In crisis lies the potential for greatness. Remember that, Fia. That's the lesson of faith. That's the lesson of *Imani*."

"Faith," Fia whispered. " '. . . *the evidence of things not seen*.' Faith is believing in something you can't see?"

"Yes, Fia, faith is believing in the *good* things, even when we can't see them." Nana Bea continued, "Faith is a belief in your heart that right is stronger than wrong and that good is stronger than evil. When we have faith, we believe that there is a seed of goodness, even in the worst situations. . . . In crisis lies the potential for greatness."

"In crisis lies the potential for greatness," Fia repeated, thinking that *Imani* was the hardest lesson of all.

Questions for Readers from **The Faith Story**

Discuss the questions below.
Write your responses to each question in two or three sentences.

1. What does the word *cycle* mean? In your own words, explain the water cycle that is described toward the beginning of **The Faith Story.**

2. In **The Faith Story,** why is Fia afraid to go to church? What would you say to Fia to help her solve this unusual problem?

3. In Nana Bea's story, who were the children of Earth? Who were the children of Sky?

4. **The Faith Story** is named "How Butterflies Came to Be." If you had to give this story another name, what would you name it?

5. What was the sequence of events that led to the crisis for the children of Earth and Sky? List the events in the order in which they occurred.

6. What caused the Spirit of the Wind to scare the Earth and Sky children into silence? As a result of the silence, what happened?

7. In what two or three ways can you compare and contrast the meeting between the Earth children and the Sky children before and after the Spirit of the Wind scared them into being quiet?

8. In your opinion, what were the most important two or three points of the eldest baobab's speech? What lessons do you think we can learn from the eldest baobab about how we can solve problems in our daily lives? What lessons can we learn from the tiny thistle?

9. Toward the beginning of **The Faith Story** Nana Bea says, "When you have faith, Fia, you can live…" How do you think Nana Bea would have finished this statement if Fia had not interrupted her? What does faith mean to you? Write your own statement(s).

10. What happens to your worries and fears when you practice **faith in action**? Create a problem chart. In one complete sentence, describe a problem that is bothering you. Make two columns. In the first column, list two or three things that worry you or that make you feel afraid when you think about the problem. In the second column, list all the things that you can do that show you have faith to solve the problem. This is your **faith in action** list. Read and reread your **faith in action** list. Then do the things on your list—act on your faith!

11. What two or three lessons did Fia learn in **The Faith Story**?

12. What is the most important lesson for *you* in **The Faith Story**? Why?

CHARACTER DEVELOPMENT ACTIVITIES FOR **THE FAITH STORY**

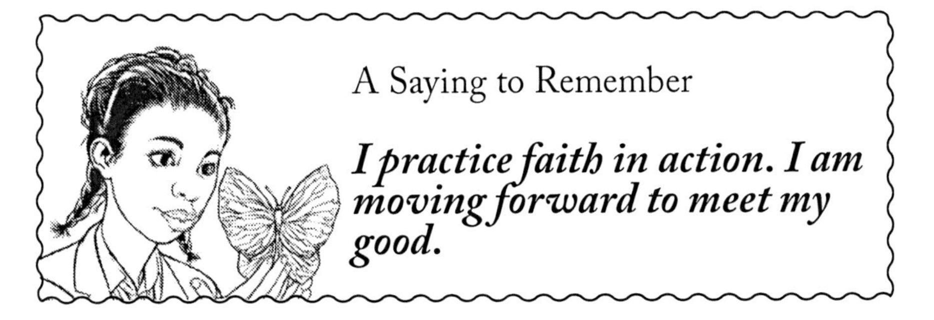

1. Copy the saying to remember for **The Faith Story.** Put the saying in a special place.

2. Memorize the saying and think about what it means to you.

3. Write a 5- to 8-sentence paragraph that describes how you relate the saying to your own life. Include the following in your paragraph:

    a. What this saying means to you

    b. How you will use this saying to improve yourself in one or more of the following areas: your health, your schoolwork, your attitude, your thoughts and feelings about yourself, your relationships with others, and/or your daily behavior

    Share your paragraph with an encouraging friend or with a supportive adult.

4. Make a list of real-world tasks that you can undertake in order to make the lessons you learned in **The Faith Story** a reality in your life. See the starter list below for ideas.

   a. Speak positive and affirming words to others. Make the commitment—and make the effort—to resolve conflicts in peaceful ways.
   b. Watch your *self-talk*—the words that you say to yourself in your mind. Make the effort to speak only positive and affirming words to yourself. Positive *self-talk* can increase your confidence in life!
   c. Sing and hum inspirational songs that make you feel better about life.
   d. Ask people—adults and your friends—to tell you what they do to stay hopeful and positive. Make a list of Staying Hopeful ideas from these interviews.
   e. Practice one thing from your Staying Hopeful list each week. Resolve to make hopefulness a personal habit.

5. Take action on the real-world tasks on your list. Record your experiences in a special journal.

Character Development Reminder

***Think about it!* Silence is golden. Discover the power of silence in your life. Sit quietly, breathe deeply, and listen to your inner guide. Then move forward toward the good, even when you can't see it. Remember—"*Faith is the substance of things hoped for, the evidence of things not seen.*"**

Conclusion

Fia Feels Better

Setting: Fia's Imagination and Louisville, Kentucky

"**Nana Bea, I'll** never be able to remember everything you've taught me," Fia moaned in distress.

"You'll remember, Fia," Nana Bea assured her. "These lessons are like seeds and they will continue to grow in your mind and heart, nourishing the character of the woman you will become."

"Nana Bea, I'm 11 years old. I can't imagine being a woman. It's too far away!"

"Don't worry about it, Fia. Just keep cultivating your talents. Develop your gifts so you can be your own best self. You'll be a fine woman, Fia," Nana Bea said proudly.

Then she said, "Fia, I want you to cup your hands in front of your chest."

"Why, Nana?"

Nana Bea's voice was getting softer. "Just do it, Fia."

Fia put her hands in front of her chest like she was saying

her prayers. Then she opened her palms and moved them forward, making a little cup with her hands as Nana Bea instructed. Then something extraordinary happened! Nana Bea began to transform. She became smaller and smaller until she looked exactly like the butterfly drawing on Fia's assignment book.

Then the butterfly flew toward Fia and landed on her outstretched hands. Fia smiled as she looked at the beautiful butterfly, which rested lightly on her palms. Fia felt peaceful and serene.

The butterfly whispered, "Fia, it's time for you to move toward your new future, but first, you have to release the past. Let go, Fia. Let go."

Then the butterfly floated upward, her wings glowing with a soft radiance that made Fia think of stained-glass windows in church. Fia felt a stirring of joy in her heart. She knew that she was witnessing something very special—something wondrous.

"What's happening?" Fia asked, looking at the beautiful butterfly in awe-struck amazement.

"It's my time to go, child. But don't worry. Remember, death is a natural part of life. That's how we all are made." The butterfly spoke so softly that Fia had to listen with her heart to hear her. Fia watched as the glow from the butterfly's wings stretched across the sky into an amazingly beautiful rainbow.

Fia looked at the rainbow and felt calm and peaceful. Her heart opened as she watched the lovely colors sparkling against the deepening blue of the early evening sky. Then the rainbow—and the butterfly—began to fade.

Thoughts, tumbling over each other, began to race through Fia's mind. "Nana Bea is leaving me! She's really going! What will I do without Nana Bea?" Fia felt afraid. She shouted in dismay, "Nana Bea! Don't go! Don't leave me! I have another question. Don't leave me, Nana! I have another question!" Fia stretched her arms, desperately trying to catch the fading rainbow.

"I have another question!" Fia repeated, flailing her arms wildly and turning her head from side to side.

"Oh, thank goodness! She's moving," the woman said. "Don't worry. You're okay, honey. You're okay."

"Where . . . where am I?" Fia asked the woman, who was gently patting her hand. The woman was wearing layers of colorful, gauzy clothing—golden yellow with lovely lavender and soft-red highlights—that shimmered beautifully in the bright lights. "You remind me of somebody but I can't remember who," Fia said, blinking her eyes. "Who are you? And where am I?"

"Why, I'm Mrs. Jewel and you're in my dance school," said the woman. "You had a pretty hard fall out there, but we brought you in here and thank goodness you seem to be all right." Fia sat up slowly and looked around.

"Well, aren't you *pretty*," Mrs. Jewel said. "And just look at that dancer's neck! I think you have landed in the right place, my dear."

Fia looked hard at Mrs. Jewel. "Dancer's neck?" she thought. "Pretty?" Fia looked around. "Look at that!" she whispered as she saw her reflection in a huge floor-to-ceiling mirror. It was as if she were seeing herself for the very first time.

Then Fia saw colorful costumes hanging on racks. She saw framed photographs of dancers. The photographs were incredible! She saw pictures of the Nicholas Brothers flying in the air. She saw pictures of Katherine Dunham and her dancers posing dramatically. They looked like magnificent brown statues. She saw pictures of Ward Flemyng and Thelma Hill with members of their New York Negro Ballet Company. Some of the women were sitting on the shoulders of strong-looking men. Some of the women were standing on their toes! They all looked proud and beautiful.

"Wow!" Fia whispered. Her eyes got wide. "This is amazing, marvelous, awesome . . ." Fia said, running out of words for a moment. Then she said, "Hey! I can see my vocabulary words!" Fia felt safe, like she belonged here. "Sanctuary," she whispered.

Then three girls rushed over. "Fia! Fia! Are you all right?" they asked, talking all at once. "We got off the school bus and there you were on the sidewalk! You were so still! It's a good thing you fell here, near Mrs. Jewel's dance school. Are you all right, Fia? Are you all right?"

Fia touched her neck. She turned her head from side to side. She moved her shoulders and stretched her arms and legs. She wriggled her fingers and wiggled her toes. Then, little by little, Fia stood up.

"Well, Fia?" the girls repeated. "Are you all right?"

Fia looked at the concerned faces of the three girls. She looked at Mrs. Jewel. She looked at Mrs. Jewel's dance studio with its colorful costumes and incredible photographs. Then Fia did a shimmy-shimmy-jump-jump and three little hops, watching her reflection in the big mirror. A big smile lit up her face and her eyes sparkled as she repeated the movement. As Fia danced, the lights and colors in Mrs. Jewel's studio created a radiance that entered Fia's heart, driving out all of her worries and fears.

"Yes!" Fia exclaimed. "I am feeling all right now!" Fia stretched her arms wide. She felt like hugging the entire world. "Yes!" she repeated. "***Now*** I am feeling all right!"

The End

Questions for Readers from **The Conclusion**

Discuss the questions below.
Write your responses to each question in two or three sentences.

1. What four words from Fia's vocabulary assignment does she think of when she wakes up in the dance studio? What does Fia say about these words?

2. What is happening to Nana Bea at the end of Fia's dream? What does Nana Bea say to comfort Fia?

3. When Fia comes out of her dream, she wakes up in Mrs. Jewel's dance school. What does Mrs. Jewel's dance school look like? Give at least three or four details.

4. The **Conclusion** is named "Fia Feels Better." If you had to give the **Conclusion** another name, what would you name it?

5. Create a time line showing three to five emotions that Fia experiences in the **Conclusion**. What does the time line teach you about the nature of emotions?

6. When does Fia feel most upset in the **Conclusion?** Name at least two things that cause Fia to feel so upset.

7. In what two or three ways can you compare and contrast Mrs. Jewel, the dance teacher, to Nana Bea?

8. Why do you think that Fia feels like she really belongs in Mrs. Jewel's dance school? Think of a place—real or imagined—where you feel that you really belong. Where is that place? What does it look like? What are the colors? What are the sounds? What do you feel like when you are in that place?

9. If there were a Part II to *Fia and the Butterfly*, what would you want to happen? Why? (*Share your ideas with Dr. Gaines through her Web site—www.taylor-gaines.com*)

10. What nine or more lessons does Fia learn in *Fia and the Butterfly?* Make a story map or a game board that traces the journey that Fia takes beginning with the **Introduction**, through the seven stories, and in the **Conclusion.** On your story map or game board, record the lessons that Fia learns. Also record how you relate those lessons to your own life.

11. What two or three lessons did Fia learn in the **Conclusion?**

12. What is the most important lesson for *you* in the **Conclusion?** Why?

Additional Information

Additional Information

Reflections

My aim in writing *Fia and the Butterfly: 7 Stories for Character Education* was to pass on the values that were passed on to me and to other members of my generation by our parents, relatives, neighbors, teachers, ministers, and other significant role models as we grew up in what has been called the Negro South of the 1950s and 1960s. Those values, like the values that we celebrate during *Kwanzaa*, are based on the following: a love for and a dedication to making things better for our children, a respect for our elders, an understanding of the importance of learning and education, a commitment to community uplift, and an abiding faith in our Creator. These enduring values are based on the traditional lifeways of our Mother Africa.

I had been telling many of the stories in *Fia and the Butterfly* for years, but I saw and felt them in a new way in the summer of 1999 when I traveled to Kenya, East Africa. There, the stories took on a new life as I met people and saw places I had seen before only in my imagination. It was wonderful! When I returned from Kenya, I wanted to write about my experiences, but I struggled to think of a way to organize my stories. By a marvelous coincidence, *Kiswahili*, a language commonly spoken in Kenya, is also the language of *Kwanzaa*. I decided to organize my Kenya stories around the *Nguzo Saba*, the Seven Principles that we celebrate during *Kwanzaa*.

> **Note:** Although the *Kwanzaa* principles are based on the values and lifeways of traditional Africa, these principles are important for all people, not just African Americans.

I am pleased with the success of the 2005 edition of *Fia and the Butterfly*. I have heard some lovely stories. A grandfather told me that he purchased one book, thinking that his grandchildren would read it and pass it on. When he loaned *Fia and the Butterfly* to his granddaughter, she begged him to let her keep it! He was pleased to order three more books—two to give to his other grandchildren and one to keep for himself. A mother told me that her daughter quoted a lesson from one of the stories during a conversation that the two of them were having about personal appearance and self-esteem. She was thrilled and so was I! A senior in high school told me she enjoyed reading *Fia and the Butterfly* the first time and intends to read it again. This is just what I wanted to happen! As a storyteller and as an educator, I want the stories and the lessons in *Fia and the Butterfly* to serve as a positive point of reference for our young people and for their parents and guardians, too.

I added the Questions for Readers and the Character Development Activities to this 2007 edition in order to make it easier for parents, teachers, and other concerned adults to engage young people in discussions about the stories and to help them to apply the lessons in the stories to their everyday lives. This section includes background information about *Kwanzaa* and the Civil Rights Movement and references related to the stories.

I expect that as you use the Questions for Readers and the Character Development Activities, you will generate your own ideas about how to use the stories in *Fia and the Butterfly* to teach and inspire young people. Please share your experiences and ideas with me through my Web site, www.taylor-gaines.com.

Information about *Kwanzaa*

The seven stories in *Fia and the Butterfly* help us to better understand the *Nguzo Saba,* the Seven Principles observed during the 7-day cultural celebration of *Kwanzaa.* Celebrated from December 26th through January 1st of each year, *Kwanzaa* was created in 1966 by Dr. Maulana Karenga, activist, educator, philosopher, and cultural historian. Dr. Karenga created *Kwanzaa* in order to acknowledge, build upon, and celebrate the values and lifeways of traditional Africa. In his Annual Founders Message–2004 on the Official *Kwanzaa* Web site, Dr. Karenga stated that a primary purpose of *Kwanzaa* is to increase the good in the world. *Kiswahili*, a language commonly spoken in Kenya and which has spread to other countries in East, Central, and Southern Africa, is the official language of *Kwanzaa.* Each one of the seven days of *Kwanzaa* is devoted to a different principle. Each principle helps to remind us of an important value that, when practiced consistently, will help us to improve our lives, our communities, and our world. Written below are my personal interpretations of the meaning and importance of each of the Seven Principles of *Kwanzaa.*

1. *Umoja* (oo-MO-jah) **Unity** / This principle reminds us of the importance of creating harmony in our families, our institutions, and our communities, of expressing respect for the elders and the traditional values that they represent, and of cherishing the earth that supports our lives.

2. *Kujichagulia* (koo-jee-ja-goo-LEE-ah) **Self-determination** / This principle reminds us of the importance of defining our own standards of excellence, of celebrating our own standards of beauty, of speaking our own thoughts and ideas, and of growing into our own best selves.

3. *Ujima* (oo-JEE-mah) **Collective Work and Responsibility** / This principle reminds us of the importance of building and maintaining strong families and healthy communities and of solving our problems together.

4. *Ujamaa* (oo-JAH-mah) **Cooperative Economics** This principle reminds us of the importance of sharing our time, energy, finances, and other resources with each other, and of creating useful and profitable businesses that benefit our families and our communities.

5. *Nia* (NEE-ah) **Purpose** / This principle reminds us of the importance of educating ourselves for personal excellence and self-sufficiency and of being of service to our families, our neighborhoods, and our communities in order to increase the good in the world.

6. *Kuumba* (kuh-OOM-bah) **Creativity** / This principle reminds us of the importance of developing and using our creative talents in order to make things more joyous and more beautiful in our own lives, in the lives of others, and in our surroundings.

7. *Imani* (ee-MAH-nee) **Faith** / This principle reminds us of the importance of believing in the existence of a higher power for good in the world and of translating that belief into our thinking, actions, and activities each and every day.

Although *Kwanzaa* is celebrated from December 26th through January 1st, it is my belief that we should use these principles to help us to live better lives *every* day of the year.

Information about the Civil Rights Movement

Fia is a black child growing up in the South in 1963 surrounded by the events of the Civil Rights Movement. Those were tempestuous times, full of purpose and glory, full of backlash and blood. Those were turbulent times, marked by the struggle of black people to remove the restrictions of Jim Crow, the legalized separation of the races—apartheid—right here in the United States of America.

Touched by the tenor of the times and inspired by a vision of freedom, black people rose up—black people of all ages—grown folks and children, teenagers and youth, they rose up, my Lord, black people rose up! And not just black people—people of good heart throughout the country—people, black and white, stirred by the injustices, took action. The people rose up! The people rose up, taught and led by heroes like the Rev. Fred Shuttlesworth, Ms. Fannie Lou Hamer, the Rev. Hosea Williams, the Rev. James Bevel, the Rev. C.T. Vivian, Ms. Ella Baker, Mr. A.G. Gadson, Ms. Septima Poinsette Clark, Mr. Myles Horton, and the other teachers of the Highlander Institute in Tennessee. The people rose up in a mighty movement for justice and righteousness.

Some of the leaders of that movement, like the Rev. Dr. Martin Luther King, Jr. and Ms. Rosa Parks, are still remembered today for their courage and commitment. But there were hundreds and thousands of others, whose names we do not remember, whose names we may never have heard . . . so many others, people who marched, ran freedom schools, and risked their lives so that all black people could exercise their basic rights to vote and to get a good education. . . . foot soldiers in Selma, Alabama like Ms. Amelia Boynton, Ms. Marie Foster, and Mama Lillie Brown. Young people like Stokely Carmichael, Robert Moses, Jean Wheeler Smith, David Dennis, Muriel Tillinghast, Ruby Doris Smith-Robinson, Willie Ricks, Alice Walker, Jerome Smith, Bernice Johnson Reagon, Matthew Jones, and so many others, including John Lewis and Diane Nash, students at Fisk University . . . people of hope and courage . . . people of hope and courage who could not stand by and watch the injustices without doing *something.*

Many lost their lives, were killed by cowardly and unthinking whites, terrorists who struck out in a bloody backlash, beating protestors, bombing their churches and their homes, using skin-tearing fire hoses and vicious attack dogs to beat back the demonstrators. Many people were injured. They are the walking wounded, veterans of an undeclared war within these United States. Many people were injured. And many people were killed. We lost Medgar Evers in Mississippi . . . and Chaney, Goodman, and Schwerner. We lost Jimmy Lee Jackson, Viola Liuzzo and Rev. James Reeb in Selma . . . and countless others—murdered in the South and in the North—martyrs to the cause of freedom . . . including four little girls, murdered on Sunday, September 15, 1963 in Birmingham, Alabama—murdered in Sunday School, in the Sixteenth Street Baptist Church—four little girls:

Addie Mae Collins
Denise McNair
Carole Robertson
and
Cynthia Wesley

. . . four innocent lives shattered by a bomb in Sunday School. These four little girls were murdered, and countless lives were changed forever.

GRATITUDE

I am grateful to God for inspiring me to write **Fia and the Butterfly** *and for sending me so much wonderful help along the way! I am grateful for lifelong friend, Ms. Judith C. Owens Lalude, who read and critiqued every word of the 2005 edition. I am grateful for my mentor, colleague, and friend Dr. Lorraine Monroe who gave so generously of her time and wisdom at every stage of every edition, and for the support of other co-workers at the Lorraine Monroe Leadership Institute including Ms. Judith S. Mutunga, Ms. Kim McCrae, Ms. Yvonne Bentick, Mr. Nate Higgins, Ms. Jo Ann Asciutto, Ms. Cleo Lucas, and Ms. Carrie Simpson, whose advice is always right on target.*

I am grateful for the advice and artistry of educator and actor Dr. Dorothy Carter, the voice of Nana Bea on **The Faith Story** *CD, and for the other wonderful members of the creative team including Mr. A. Dean Irby, Mr. Bob Cunningham, Mr. Warren Smith, Ms. Andrea L. Cosley, and Mr. Tom McGrath. I am grateful for the gifted team that helped to create this 2007 edition including educator Dr. Claudia Moore-Hamilton, who helped to shape the Questions for Readers and the Character Development Activities, artist, Mr. Harvey Richards, book designer, Mr. Babatunde Odesanya, proofreaders, Mr. James McCallum and Ms. Pauline Gilbert-Bader, Web site designer, Mr. Cecil Lee (www.art-alive.com), and marketing assistant, Ms. Lucinda Cross.*

I am grateful for my relatives who listened and helped, including Aunt Frances Williams, Aunt Ora Lee Gaines (deceased), Aunt Lynette (Dr. Lynette Seine Gaines, deceased), Uncle Robert and Aunt Shirley Harris, Cousins Claudine and Jesse Chatman, Cousin Debra Elaine Bailey, Cousin Faya Rose Touré, Cousin Hank Sanders, Cousin Lila Nelson and her daughter, Leah Nelson, Cousins T.D. and Marian Jordan,

Cousins Willie and Sheila Martin, and Cousin Dora Martin.

I am grateful for the support of and suggestions from enduring and newfound friends including Ms. Constance D. Anderson, Ms. Elizabeth A. Jones, Dr. Edythe Boyer Jones, Ms. Cynthia Taylor, Mr. Andi Owens, Dr. Beryl Duncan Wilson, her daughter, Afiya Wilson (who inspired Fia's name), Mr. LeRoy Griffin, Ms. Cheryl Forbes, Mr. Perry Cannon, Mr. Ronnie Davis, Dr. Esther Hyatt, and Mr. and Mrs. George Edward and Akosua Tait. I am grateful for the creative advice of Mr. Eleo Pomare, Mr. Glenn Conner, Dr. Beryle Banfield, Dr. Vivian Windley, and Mr. Selaelo Maredi and for the kind and insightful comments of Dr. John Bolling, MD, the Rev. Canon Jesse Anderson, and the Rev. C.T. Vivian.

I am grateful for Ms. Mary Kocy and Ms. Bernadette Rhames who organized the New Perspectives Program's Workshop for Writers at Bank Street College of Education. I am grateful for the encouragement of the participants and for wise guidance from workshop leader, Ms. Miriam Cohen. I am grateful for my community of friends-in-the-work in Louisville, Kentucky, especially Nana Yaa Asantewaa, Ms. Zambia Nkrumah White, and Ms. Elmer Lucille Allen.

I am grateful for the young people who critiqued my work, including students at the Frederick Douglass Academy II (FDA II)—Alfred Cabral, Janelle Garcia, Joy Gardner, Jameelah McKay, Alexis Morrison, and Schinae Peterson—who wrote comments about my manuscript in 2001 when they were in the 7th grade; Autumn Simmons who wrote comments in 2003 when she was in the 4th grade; and FDA II students Christina Cruz and Kashif Muhammad who wrote comments in 2007 when they were in the 12th grade. I am grateful for the leaders who gave them the assignments—Ms. Karole Turner Campbell and Ms. Disha Lynch, and for Autumn's mother, Ms. Adrienne Logan.

I am grateful for my teachers—from nursery school through

graduate school—who nurtured my heart and my mind, and I am grateful for the schools and colleges—especially Fisk University, my undergraduate alma mater—that served as safe places in which I could discover and develop my interests and talents.

And I am grateful for sweet memories of my wonderful, God-given parents, Mr. Lonnie William Gaines, Jr. and Mrs. Gladys Marie Harris Gaines. I am grateful for the warm and loving community of relatives, neighbors, and church folk into which I was born. I am grateful for the lessons—in history and in life—taught to me by my loving husband, Mr. Jules Easton Taylor (December 18, 1952–May 13, 1984), and for the presence of the other angelic souls who were and are a part of the ongoing struggle to bring a higher good into the world.

Finally, I am grateful for spiritual guidance from ministers and members of the churches of my childhood, youth, and young adulthood—the Pilgrim Rest A.M.E. Zion Church in Mobile, Alabama, the Broadway Temple A.M.E. Zion Church in Louisville, Kentucky, and the First Church of Religious Science in New York City under the leadership of the Rev. Dr. Stuart Grayson (deceased)—and I am grateful for all of the ministers and members of my current church, the historic Mother African Methodist Episcopal Zion Church in Harlem, New York, the Rev. Dr. Gregory Robeson Smith, Pastor.

For all of these people and for all of these opportunities, I am truly grateful to God!

References for the Stories

Armstrong, Joyce. Interview with L.M. Gaines. San Francisco, California, 1988. (Revised version of the song, *Ain't Gonna Let Nobody Turn Me 'Round*, **The Purpose Story**)

Baxley, Bill. "Why Did the F.B.I. Hold Back Evidence?" *The New York Times*, OP-ED, May 3, 2001. (Information about the murder of the 4 little girls, the historical incident during the Civil Rights Movement, referred to in the Introduction, **The Purpose Story**, and **The Faith Story**.)

Berlin, Ira, Marc Favreau, and Steven F. Miller, editors. *Remembering Slavery: African Americans Talk about their Personal Experiences of Slavery and Emancipation*. New York: The New Press in association with the Library of Congress, Washington, D.C., 1998. ("Mr. Joe's Story" in **The Purpose Story**)

Butterfly Web sites. http://www.fieldmuseum.org/butterfly/basics.htm "Butterfly Basics: Butterfly and Moth Life Cycle," and http://www.butterflyguide.co.uk/life/index.htm "The Life Cycle of a Butterfly." (**The Cooperative Economics Story**)

Cornell, Joseph. *Listening to Nature: How to Deepen Your Awareness of Nature*. Nevada City, California: Dawn Publications, 1987. (**The Unity Story**)

Harding, Vincent. *There is a River: The Black Struggle for Freedom in America*. Florida: Harcourt, Brace & Company, 1981. (**The Purpose Story**)

Karenga, Maulana. The Annual Founder's *Kwanzaa* Message, 2004. "*Kwanzaa* and the Seven Principles: Creating and Practicing Good in the World." http://www.officialkwanzaawebsite.org

Lee, Spike. *4 Little Girls: A Film by Spike Lee*. New York: HBO Productions, 1997. (The Introduction, **The Purpose Story**, and **The Faith Story**)

Lester, Julius. *Black Folktales*, "How God Made the Butterflies." New York: Grove Press, 1969. (Master storyteller Julius Lester retells this traditional black folktale about the origin of butterflies. In **The Faith Story**, I retell the story in my own way.)

Moorehead, Monica. "The FBI and the Birmingham Church Bombing," *Workers World*, July 24, 1997. http://www.4littlegirls.com/97news.htm (The Introduction)

Mullane, Deirdre, editor. *Crossing the Danger Water: Three Hundred Years of African-American Writing*. New York: Anchor Books, 1993. ("*Ain't Gonna Let Nobody Turn Me 'Round*," **The Purpose Story**)

Paulsen, Gary. *Nightjohn*. New York: Bantam Doubleday Dell Books for Young Readers, 1993. ("Mr. Joe's Story" in **The Purpose Story**)

Songs of Zion: Supplemental Worship Resources 12. Nashville, TN: Abingdon. (Excerpt from the song, *Nkosi Sikelel'i Afrika* or "Prayer for Africa" in the Introduction)

The Bible, KJV, Hebrews 11:1 (*"Now faith is the substance of things hoped for, and the evidence of things not seen"* in **The Faith Story**) and 1 Kings 19:12 (*"a still small voice"* in **The Collective Work and Responsibility Story**)

Washington, Booker T. *Up from Slavery*, 1901. http://www.bartleby.com/1004 (**The Purpose Story**)

Note: *Fia and the Butterfly* includes numerous folk sayings, proverbs, and maxims. In addition, the book contains quotations from Dr. Albert Schweitzer ("Have reverence for life" in **The Unity Story**), Mr. George Washington Carver ("Keep your eyes open to what Mother Nature has to teach you" in **The Unity Story** and "Education is the key that unlocks the golden door to freedom" in **The Purpose Story**), and the Rev. Dr. Martin Luther King, Jr. (the "content of their character" quotation that precedes the stories).

References from the Author's Visit to Kenya

Note: It was my visit to Kenya in East Africa in the summer of 1999 that contextualized my stories and compelled me to write them. Most of the organizations and places listed below can be visited on the Internet, but why not plan a trip to the Motherland to see these beautiful places for yourself?

African Quest Safaris, Tasneem and Taher Adamji, Founding Partners, http://www.africanquest.co.ke

Butterfly Breeding Station, Bamburi Forest Nature Trails, Paul Musila, Research Assistant, Mombasa, Kenya

Mwaluganje Elephant Sanctuary, Frederick Oganda, Manager, Kwale District, Kenya

Tototo Women's Group, Mombasa, Kenya

Wema Centre for Children, Mombasa, Kenya

ORDER Additional Products!

Fia and the Butterfly comes to life
through *The Faith Story* CD!

The Faith Story—the seventh story from *Fia and the Butterfly*—comes to life on an audio CD directed by A. Dean Irby and recorded by stellar actors Dr. Dorothy Carter and Andrea L. Cosley along with classic jazz musicians Bob Cunningham and Warren Smith. ***The Faith Story*** CD also contains music from Bob Cunningham's album, *Walking Bass*, featuring incredible musicians including the legendary Bross Townsend on piano. ***The Faith Story*** CD can be used in listening centers in schools, at family and community gatherings, and for dramatic presentations.

ORDER ***The Faith Story*** CD
from the Lorraine Monroe Leadership Institute (LMLI)
361 West 125th Street, Suite 2000
New York, NY 10027
PHONE: 212-531-0515 FAX: 212-531-0535
E-MAIL: LGAINES@LMLI.ORG
WEBSITE: WWW.LORRAINEMONROE.ORG

Also available through LMLI

The Monroe-Gaines Parenting Manual
by Dr. Lorraine Monroe and Dr. Lonnetta M. Gaines
and
The LMLI Booklist
compiled by the Rev. Malika Lee Whitney

I have a dream . . .

I have a dream that my book, **Fia and the Butterfly: 7 Stories for Character Education**, *will continue to grow and develop into a variety of additional publications, productions, and products including, but not limited to, the following: picture books for preschoolers and other young readers, literacy packs, curriculum guides, journals, skits, musical plays, theatrical performances, CDs, DVDs, games, dolls . . . and more stories! Dream with me! Let others know about* **Fia and the Butterfly**. *Share this book with young people. Read it for yourselves. And contact me through my Web site to share your responses and also your ideas for helping to spread the word so that others will use this book to motivate and to teach increasing numbers of our children and youth to honor, practice, and pass on our traditional values. I appreciate your support!*

I am available for Keynote Speeches, Professional Development Workshops, and Storytelling Performances based on the stories and ideas in *Fia and the Butterfly: Seven Stories for Character Education*. Contact me by e-mail or through my Web site. I look forward to hearing from you!

Lonnetta M. Taylor-Gaines

E-mail: taylor-gaines@verizon.net

Web site: www.taylor-gaines.com

NOTES

NOTES

DATE DUE

BRODART, CO. Cat. No. 23-221-003

Printed in the United States
113782LV00001B/272/A